The Thirteenth Princess

HARPER

An Imprint of HarperCollinsPublishers

The Thirteenth Princess

DIANE ZAHLER

The Thirteenth Princess
Copyright © 2010 by Diane Zahler
Page 159: from "First Look" by John Clare, public domain
Page 160: from "The Princess" by Alfred, Lord Tennyson, public domain
Page 160: from "Epitaph on the Monument of Sir William Dyer at
Colmworth, 1641" by Lady Catherine Dyer, public domain
Page 191: from "Damned Women" by Charles Baudelaire. Original French
poem is public domain; author has supplied her own translation of the
poem.

Library of Congress Cataloging-in-Publication Data
Zahler, Diane.
    The thirteenth princess / Diane Zahler. — 1st ed.
        p.   cm.
    Summary: Zita, cast aside by her father and raised as a kitchen maid,
learns when she is nearly twelve that she is the thirteenth princess and
that her sisters love her, and so when she learns they are victims of an evil
enchantment, she desperately tries to save them. Inspired by the Grimm fairy
tale, "The twelve dancing princesses."
    ISBN 978-0-06-182498-2 (trade bdg.)
    ISBN 978-0-06-182499-9 (lib. bdg.)
    [1. Fairy tales.   2. Princesses—Fiction.   3. Sisters—Fiction.
4. Household employees—Fiction.   5. Fathers and daughters—Fiction.
6. Magic—Fiction.]   I. Title.
PZ8.Z17Thi   2010   2009014575
[Fic]—dc22   CIP
                                                                      AC

Typography by Joel Tippie
10 11 12 13 14   CG/RRDB   10 9 8 7 6 5 4 3 2 1
❖
First Edition

Acknowledgments

I would like to thank the following:

*Maria Gomez and Barbara Lalicki, for their
enthusiasm and inspired editing*

*Jan and Stan Zahler, for the weekly trips
to the library that started it all*

*Debra and Arnie Cardillo, for their moral
and professional support*

Shani Chamberlain, for her ideas and encouragement

Nick Scudamore, for his perceptive suggestions

Lisa Herb, for her generous legal expertise

My family, for their unwavering belief in me

Philip Sicker, for everything

For Betty Sicker—
our beloved Babes

Contents

1. In Which I Am Born 3

2. In Which the Dumbwaiter Is Discovered 16

3. In Which I Get to Know My Sisters 30

4. In Which I Meet a Witch 52

5. In Which a Change Takes Place 68

6. In Which I Take Action 96

7. In Which I Go on a Journey 124

8. In Which I Dance 136

9. In Which Help Is Sought 148

10. In Which Help Arrives...................................166

11. In Which the Great Wave Breaks.................188

12. In Which There Is an Unmasking 202

13. In Which My Story Does Not End................ 230

Chapter 1

In Which I Am Born

y name is Zita, and I am the thirteenth of thirteen princesses. My twelve sisters have become the subject of legend, even in faraway kingdoms, but I am sure that you have never heard of me.

I first heard the tale of my birth from Cook, who was my friend and my confidante, when I was no more than seven years old. She had just showed me how to roll out a circle of dough for pie crust that didn't stick to the rolling pin, when I brought myself to ask the question that had been on my mind for some time: "Cook, where is my mother?"

Her round, flushed face became very serious, and she put down her rolling pin, dusted off her floury hands, and came to sit beside me at the long wooden table.

"I have been waiting for you to ask," she said. "You must listen as I tell you, and you must not interrupt."

Solemnly, I nodded.

"Your mother was the queen, the wife of our king," Cook began. Immediately I interrupted.

"What are you talking about?" I demanded. "She was the queen? *Our* queen? Do you mean that King Aricin is my father—that horrid man? Wait—do you mean that the princesses are my *sisters*?"

Cook glared at me and reached for the rolling pin, and I ducked instinctively, though I knew she would never so much as tap me with it.

Before Cook could go on, the underbutler, Burle, appeared at the kitchen door for his midmorning tea. He was a short man with the face of a weasel and whiskers to match, and I despised him. Whenever he entered a room, I left, so I took the opportunity to scurry under his arm and out of the kitchen as Cook hurried to put the kettle on.

In an upper hallway I found Chiara, the housekeeper, who loved to gossip. I hoped she would tell me more. She paused in her dusting when she saw me.

"Do you not have a task to do, Zita?" she scolded me.

"If not, I can find you one quick enough!"

"No, wait," I begged. "Cook has told me something amazing. Is it true? Are the princesses my sisters?"

Chiara's beady eyes softened. "True enough," she told me.

"Then the queen—the queen was my mother?"

Chiara gave a bark of laughter. "You'd never know it to look at you, but it is so!"

I could hardly take this in, it was so strange and wondrous. I was a princess! No matter that my hands were reddened from washing dishes and the ends of my hair scorched from working too near the kitchen fire. I was related to the twelve beautiful, golden-haired girls I saw only from a distance, graceful and lovely in their embroidered gowns and delicate jewels. To think about it, I sat behind a potted plant, where no one would bother me, and soon more questions occurred to me. I went back to Cook for answers, knowing that Burle would have finished his tea and departed.

"What did my mother look like?" I wanted to know.

"Oh, Queen Amara was as beautiful as ever a queen could be," Cook told me, sprinkling herbs into the soup. She described the queen's silvery hair, and her eyes as blue as a spring-fed lake. My mother loved the king, Cook said, and he adored her. Their marriage was a cause for great rejoicing in the kingdom, for the king was nearly forty by then and had despaired of ever finding a wife. He would not marry for heirs alone, nor for convenience, but waited for true love. He had many dalliances as he waited, of course, for he was a handsome man in those days.

I could not help myself. "What is a dalliance?" I asked.

Cook's red face turned even redder, and she harrumphed in the way she had when she did not want to answer a question.

"He was well liked, is what I meant," Cook responded. "Various princesses longed for him, and many others— from ladies in waiting to serving maids—caught his eye. But he bided his time, and he found the love he sought with your mother."

Within a year, Cook told me, the queen was pregnant. The king had hoped for a son, but when a daughter was born, he was pleased nonetheless. On her naming day, Mother clothed the baby in a silken dress embroidered with pearls and gold, and the king named her Aurelia, his golden one. "All our children shall have names beginning with A, like their mother," the king said fondly. They delighted in the child's calm smiles and sparkling blue eyes. Her hair came in golden blond, and even as a baby she was beautiful, like the queen.

"That is the princess Aurelia?" I asked.

Cook nodded, allowing the interruption.

I hugged myself in pleasure. The most beautiful, the kindest of princesses—and she was my oldest sister!

"Your father loved your sister Aurelia so much that at her birth, he banned magic from the kingdom, fearing that an evil witch might curse her at her christening, as has happened so often," Cook informed me. I had heard tales of princesses cursed at their birth by wicked or jealous witches, and I thought this a very wise and loving thing for a father to do.

The soup that Cook had forgotten to stir boiled over at that point, and she blamed me and banished me to the upper floors again. This time, I hid behind a piece of statuary and waited. I knew the princesses—my sisters!—would soon be going out for their daily exercise—a walk, or a ride on horseback, or a turn about the lake in their little rowboats. Sure enough, a few moments later I heard their cheerful voices and the sound of their heels clattering down the stairs. Nurse led them, and to my joy Aurelia was last in line. As she passed by me, I stepped out and plucked at her skirt, whispering, "Princess!"

Aurelia stopped and turned, and her fair face broke into a smile of genuine pleasure.

"Little Zita!" she said. "How pretty your curls look today!"

I pulled at my red ringlets, which I hated.

"I have always wished for curls," Aurelia told me. "Do you know what I have to do to curl my hair?"

I shook my head.

She laughed. "It is an endless process—and sometimes painful. You are lucky!"

I was tempted to go on talking of hair and curls, but I needed to know something.

"Princess," I said hesitantly, "I have heard—is it true?—do you know—that you and I are sisters?"

I waited for her to gasp in shock, or laugh at me, or look at me with disdain. She did none of those things. Instead she took my hands quickly in hers.

"Yes, Zita. I do know this," she said in a low voice. "We all do. And I am so glad that you know it now! We've hated that we've had to keep it secret from you."

"Princess Aurelia!" Nurse called from below us.

Aurelia looked hurriedly around, and I could see worry in her face. "But I cannot talk now—I must join the others." And before I could say another word, she squeezed my hands, whirled about, and hurried off to catch up with the rest. I watched her go, puzzled by the mystery that seemed to surround our relationship. But still, I was so happy. Just an hour before, I had been nothing more than a kitchen maid, with no relations, no real friend but Cook. Now I had sisters—twelve of them!

For a while I was content simply to know this and to watch my sisters and imagine myself with them. As I grew older, though, I began to have more and more questions. No one seemed to want to tell me everything, but by the time I was eleven I had pieced together the story of my sisters' births from tales told by Chiara, Cook, and Salina, Bethea, and Dagman, the maids with whom I shared a room. They told me that soon after Aurelia was born—very soon, according to the midwives—Mother was again with child. This time she delivered twins, both girls, both blue-eyed and yellow-haired. The king was a little distressed, but he masked it well. He proclaimed the twins Alanna, because he thought her handsome, and Ariadne, because her steady gaze was a chain that clasped his heart, and he smiled as if he meant it. After dinner each day, he visited the nursery and played with Aurelia and rocked the twins. Chiara said to me in a rare sentimental moment, "I remember thinking that I had never seen such a happy family."

A year later, Mother was brought to bed again. Again, a girl, Althea, issued forth. The king scowled this time when he heard the news. Adena came next, then Asenka, and then another set of twins, Amina and Alima. By the time these twins were born, the king no longer appeared at the ceremonies, and Mother was thin, approaching gaunt, and tired, though she was only twenty-five.

When Akila, the ninth child, was born, the king was out hunting, and he did not return until two days later. Whispers began in the palace about his distress over the unending line of girls. After the springtime birth of Allegra, and again when Mother bore Asmita, the king raged through the gardens, scattering servants before him like chaff before a wind.

The twelfth baby was born after a hard, long labor, and she went nameless for a week. The castle buzzed with the idea of a princess without a name. Then a kitchen maid suggested the name Anisa to the cook, who repeated it to a downstairs maid. The downstairs maid whispered the name to an upstairs maid, who left it written on a scrap of paper in the nursery. When Nurse found the paper, she brought it to Mother, and wearily Mother accepted the name, never guessing that it had been the name of the kitchen maid's cat.

The king cursed when he found out the baby was a girl. "No more children," he proclaimed, and he stopped visiting Mother's room. Mother did not recover fully from Anisa's birth; the doctors were at a loss to find the problem. "I think," Cook said to me wistfully, "that sadness made her weaken and fail."

After I learned about Anisa, I stopped asking for a time, fearful of what I would find out. Finally, though, I had to know. I went to Cook, and she told me the last part of the terrible tale, which began when our nearest neighbor, King Damon, visited our castle. Our guests had grown few over the years. Once, Cook said, our court was a place of great fun, and nobles vied for the invitations that the king and Mother issued for their Twelfth Night and May Day festivals. There were no more of these, but still the occasional wandering king, bored with peace in his own kingdom, might happen by. King Damon brought with him his family—his wife, frumpy Queen Eleanora, and his four sons. Four sons! Aurelia, Alanna, Ariadne, and Althea, now eleven, ten, and nine years old, were thrilled, but the king could hardly bear it. To have to entertain a man who had not one heir but four was too much for him. The four boys played with his older daughters, laughing and dancing about the parquet floor of the drawing room, and the king watched them in silence as he drank glass after glass of wine. After the jesters and tumblers had finished and the guests had stumbled off to bed, he made his way down the long-unused hall to Mother's room. In a fury, he hammered on her door, and when she rushed to open it, he cried out, "I must have a son!"

Now Cook took my hands in hers, and I felt from the dampness of her palms that I would not like this part of the story.

"Nine months later," she told me, "on a day so hot and oppressive that even to move was to sweat, your mother's labor began. This time, the king paced the floor outside the room in agony. Doctors came and went, looking ever more worried. If I had not known that magic was banned from the kingdom, I would have said that a bad enchantment was at work that day. The heat grew, and at last the sky darkened and cracked open with lightning."

Cook paused in her story, and I held my breath, caught between dread and anticipation. "A moment later there came a scream so high and horrifying that the glass in the labor room's windows cracked. The king rushed inside to find a wild scene of frantic doctors and midwives, trying to staunch the blood that flowed from your mother. In the midst of mayhem, a baby's cry sounded, and the king scrambled to find the source of the cry."

She paused again, and I trembled, for I knew what she would say.

"It was a girl," she told me gently. "It was you."

I wept then, knowing that I was the thirteenth daughter born to a king who wanted only a son. In every tale I know, the number thirteen is bad luck. If thirteen come to dinner, another invitation is sent out quickly, another place laid. When houses are numbered, thirteen is always skipped. I felt that I was the unluckiest person in the world. My tears fell still harder when Cook said, "Your mother died that night, my child. It was through no fault of yours, but simply from exhaustion and loss of blood."

"If it was not my fault," I sobbed, "then why does the king—my father—hate me?"

Cook sighed and wiped my face with the towel she kept always threaded through her apron strings.

"He was wild with grief and despair," she told me. "He loved your mother so, though he seemed to have forgotten that over time. But I am sure he does not blame you or hate you."

Cook was overcome and did not want to go on, but I sensed that there was more to the tale. I went in search of Chiara and found her moving from room to room upstairs. Her keys rattled on their long chain as she surveyed each chamber, making sure fires were lighted, windows sparkled, and drapes were drawn or open as the king preferred. I scuttled along behind her as quickly as I could.

"Oh yes, it's all true," she said, her dour face glowing with the pleasure of telling tales. "When he looked at you, his lip twisted up the way it is now; and so it has stayed. And before he left the labor room, he said to Nurse, 'I never want to see this child. Place her with the servants. Keep her from my eyes. She has killed her mother, and my hope.'"

I gasped.

Chiara went on. "Nurse protested," she told me, "saying, 'She is just a baby. Her mother's death is no fault of hers! Please, Your Majesty, at least give the babe a name!'

"But your father laughed and said, 'A name? She shall not be Arabella, or Alcantha, or Ava. She is no true daughter of mine. Call her Zita, after the patron saint of servants, and keep her with the servants, out of my sight.' And then he fled the room.

"And so," Chiara finished, "here you are, and there he is, and what can be done? Oh, child, stop your sniveling and do get out of my way!" And she swept away from me, leaving me to try to make some sense of my world, which I no longer recognized at all.

I wandered to a mirror in the hallway and stood staring at my reflection. I did not see the face of a princess. I was streaked with tears, and flour where Cook had wiped my face, and some dirt as well. Princesses were not filthy; my sisters were always clean and fresh. I was not blond, nor blue-eyed. My sisters all had straight hair like silk, in colors from silver to gold, and their eyes were aquamarine and the color of sky and violet and every other shade blue might be. But my hair sprang curled and red, and my eyes were as green as wild thyme.

As I stood there looking at myself, I saw suddenly another face in the glass behind me. I had been so intent that I had not realized the king—my father—had come up behind me. I gave a little shriek and turned, curtsying as best I could. I did not dare to meet his eyes, but I could see his twisted lip and perpetual scowl.

"What are you doing up here, Zita?" he asked me. To my ears, still ringing with the story I'd been told, his voice sounded harsh and accusing.

"I am sorry," I said fearfully. "I am—I just—"

He looked at me a moment longer, and at last I dared to meet his eyes. To my surprise they were as green as mine and did not quite match his scowl. They did not seem angry to me, only sad, and I felt less afraid.

"Go," he said at last, and I ran, my tears dried and my heart suddenly full. As terrible as my birth had been, as cold as the king was to me, he was my father, and the princesses were my sisters. At last, at last, I truly felt that I had a family.

Chapter 2

In Which the Dumbwaiter Is Discovered

illed with a confidence that came from my new awareness of my past and my place, I began to get to know my sisters. I made sure that our paths crossed frequently. Sometimes when the girls were out boating on the lake, I would pass by on an errand, and we would shout and wave to each other. Or some of them might be out riding when I was in the woods collecting morels, and we would stop and talk for a moment. Aurelia especially made a point of speaking briefly to me when our father was not around. I thrilled to every moment of contact, as fleeting as such moments were.

My feelings about the palace where we lived had changed as well. I was still a servant and did servant's work there, it is true. I dusted and swept, made pastries with Cook, hunted mushrooms in the woods, and looked after the chickens, but I did these jobs gladly now, with the knowledge that the palace I tended was, in a small way, my own.

One early spring day, when I was on the far side of the lake gathering wild strawberries, I looked up at the palace, daydreaming and marveling at its beauty. Father had it built over a wide stream, almost a river, held up by marble supports. The stream was where he had met my mother as she boated with her aunt, whom she was visiting from a distant kingdom. So strong was his attachment to my mother, and to the place where they first saw each other, that he insisted the stream itself become their home.

The palace was made of pink stone that shone in the dawn and dusk light. It was not large, as it was hard to build outward over the stream, but instead it rose high, with towers and lacy minarets reaching toward the sky. It seemed to float above the water, and its pink stone and marble were reflected below so that you could not be sure which was the real palace, the one above the water or the one that seemed to rest amid the lily pads. It was even more beautiful at night. Cook had told me that while my mother was alive, and a party was planned, the torches on the turrets were lit and tiny lights were placed along the crenellations. Then truly it seemed like a fairy palace, when the lights danced above and below in the night breeze.

What Father had not known was that as the years passed, the stream would gradually cease to flow, and a lake would form, its stagnant waters lapping around the mossy marble pilings. The palace itself grew damp, especially in the lower reaches. The walls dripped with moisture on humid days, and there were four servants whose job was entirely to scrub the greenish mold off the walls as it crept upward from the lake. We had few older workers in the palace, for as our servants aged, their joints stiffened in the damp. Only Nurse remained with us past the age of fifty, and she could endure the pain of arthritic hands and knees only because of her devotion to my sisters.

From where I stood I could see my sisters' tower window, and I squinted to try to make out their figures through the glass. Their room and the other family rooms were at the top of the palace, and below that were the servants' quarters, where I slept. Even three floors above the lake, they were a little chilly and damp, and we had to change the stuffing in our mattresses every few months, or it smelled like rotting fruit.

On the next floor down were the staterooms, where Father did business and met with officials and royalty from other kingdoms. They were sumptuous and stately (though damp), hung with tapestries and furnished with chairs and benches cushioned in velvet and tables of inlaid woods in intricate patterns.

The kitchen with its attached pantry was on the lowest level of the palace, but it was less damp than the rest of that floor because the fires burned there continuously, drying out the air. It was the only usable room on that level. The others were originally intended as servants' bedrooms and storerooms, but the servants who slept there soon developed infections of the lungs and fungus between their toes, and any goods stored there would shortly be rotted and covered with mold. Once I saw a rat in one of these rooms, and I ran screaming and crying to Cook. There was something about rats that terrified me—their nasty, beady eyes, their long, naked tails. I could not bear even to think of them.

Lost in thought, I started when Cook shouted from the land bridge, "Zita! Stop your dreaming and bring those berries in!" Her loud voice echoed across the lake, and I snapped to attention, grabbed my basket, and ran back through the brambles that snatched at my skirt and scratched my bare arms.

The berries were to be part of a magnificent dessert,

a strawberry cream layer cake, for tonight was an occasion. The eldest of my sisters, especially Aurelia, were of a marriageable age by now, and Father had invited King Tobin of Blaire and his son, Prince Regan, to dine. The kitchen staff had been commanded to make unusual delicacies, and I had heard my sisters twittering with excitement for days. After the cake was in the oven, Cook sent me upstairs to dust. I came across Aurelia in the upper-floor hallway as I flicked the duster here and there, her usually pale skin pink and her hair and dress elaborate.

"You look beautiful," I said shyly.

She blushed still more. "Why, thank you, Zita!" she replied.

"Are you going to dine with the prince?"

"I am," she said. "I, and Alanna, Ariadne, and Althea. I believe that Father intends for him to choose one of us."

"To marry?" I asked, fascinated.

"Yes indeed," Aurelia replied, smiling.

"But why has the king waited so long?" I asked bluntly.

Aurelia laughed. "He does not like to entertain," she reminded me. "And I truly think he had forgotten how very ancient I was, until my name-day celebration last month!" But her voice was light as she said this, for she knew she was still young and lovely.

"I hope you like the prince well, then!" I said daringly, and Aurelia laughed.

"I hope he likes *me* well, dear Zita!" She reached out and touched me on the shoulder as she passed, and I nearly swooned with happiness.

Already the staterooms were gleaming, so I wandered down the hallway to the one room at the far end whose great oaken door was kept locked. For years I had wondered about it. That day the staff was in such an uproar that Chiara had left her great chain of keys unattended on a table in the hall, a most remarkable occurrence. Without hesitation I picked up the chain and tried key after key in the door, looking nervously around with each attempt to be sure I wasn't seen. Finally one fit, the door unlatched, and I pushed it open, wincing as it squeaked after years of disuse.

I was astonished to find an enormous empty space, hung with large, moldering tapestries. The room boasted a floor of inlaid wood that might once have shone beautifully but now was dull from neglect. I wandered around, peering at the weavings on the wall in the dim light. The windows were curtained with great falls of moth-eaten maroon velvet, and my eyes could barely trace the figures woven into the hangings. I made out a court of dancing maidens, a unicorn, a dragon.

In each of the tapestries was the same figure, a lovely woman with a sheaf of silver-gold hair. My mother, I surmised, and I stood long gazing at her faded beauty on the wall.

Sneaking back out, I placed the chain of keys exactly where I had found it, returned to the kitchen, and ventured to ask Cook about the room.

"That's the ballroom," she said shortly. "Hasn't been used in . . . oh, I don't know how long. A decade, at least. Used to be . . ." Her voice trailed off, and I waited expectantly for tales of grand balls that had been held there. But Cook's attention was on the bread, and she brushed me aside as if I had been a fly buzzing around her food.

That night I passed the peas, dressed in a starched and spotless white apron. I was able to observe the meeting of my sisters and Prince Regan, who was as dark as they were fair, and as handsome as any prince should be. As thrilled as they were at the prospect, when they met him they seemed struck dumb. He kissed their hands and attempted conversation when they sat at table.

"Princess Aurelia," he said, "do you play an instrument?"

Across the table, Aurelia sat with eyes downcast and did not answer. Father's brow furrowed at her rudeness.

"I love to ride, myself," the prince addressed Althea,

who sat beside him. "Do you enjoy riding, Princess?"

Again the downcast eyes, and silence.

Poor Prince Regan became very flustered, and his father and mine took up the conversation, but the dinner ended soon and awkwardly, without my sisters having spoken a single word or raised their eyes from the table.

My father raged that night, but my sisters had no explanation for their behavior. Appalled by his daughters' lack of manners, Father brought in a deportment instructor to teach them how to behave in social situations. I thought Master Beolagh a very silly man, obsessed with propriety and manners. I brought tea to the room during one of the lessons, and after observing his teaching, I felt glad for once that I was not a true princess, forced to endure such tedium as learning to eat soup while balancing a book on my head.

Another prince came a few weeks later, and I heard from Chiara that the same thing occurred—silence, confusion, anger. "Those girls are spoiled rotten," she said sourly. "A royal prince is not good enough for them!" After that, my father did not invite any more suitors, and my sisters spent more time in their bedchamber, alone.

Although they were princesses and each should have had her own bedroom, they preferred to sleep all together in a long room with a sloping roof. Less damp and drafty than the rest of the palace, it had a fireplace at each end and six large beds on each long wall. The mattresses were plump and comfortable, the bedclothes were silk, and the quilts were patchworked velvet, each of a different color. There were beautiful Arabian carpets on the floor, cushioning my sisters' delicate feet from the cold tile and warming the place with color.

I loved that room. It was there that my sisters gossiped and combed one another's hair, discussed upcoming birthdays, swayed before mirrors, and practiced their dance steps in the spaces between the beds. I longed to go there, to spend time with my sisters. I walked past whenever I could find time and waved to whichever girls were inside, and they waved back. We all feared our father's wrath, though, if he should see us together, for as the years passed he grew not less bitter about my mother's death, but more.

It was my eighth sister, Alima, the adventurous one, who one day hid in the bedroom's huge closet during a game of hide-and-seek and discovered a false back to the space. She removed it and found a dumbwaiter there. We had dumbwaiters that ran between the kitchen and the dining hall, to bring up the food while it was still hot and bring down the dirtied dishes without breaking them. Nobody knew about this hidden dumbwaiter, though. It ran from the back of the closet in the princesses' bedchamber down to the pantry beside the kitchen, opening in a space behind the sacks of potatoes. My sisters were thrilled by the discovery, for it meant that they could sneak into the kitchen late at night and remove any sweets or pastries that had been left out. This befuddled poor Cook, who began taking the blame for losing large quantities of pie and cake that were intended for the king's table.

I was ignorant of the existence of the dumbwaiter until one afternoon when I was alone in the kitchen peeling potatoes for a galette. Cook was upstairs in her room with a headache, and I was shocked to see Aurelia come into the kitchen, for the princesses almost never ventured belowstairs.

"What are you doing here?" I asked, far more rudely than I intended, but Aurelia did not take offense.

"I have just a minute, Zita," she said with a furtive air. "Can I trust you to keep a secret?"

"Oh, yes!" I cried, and clapped a hand over my mouth as Aurelia shushed me.

"Tonight," she whispered, "when everyone has gone to sleep, go into the pantry and wait."

"But why?" I demanded.

"You will see," she said mysteriously, and swept out of the room.

I was twitchy with excitement all afternoon. That night, when Salina, Bethea, and Dagman slept, I crept out and down to the kitchen pantry. There I hid, wrapped in a flour sack, dozing and starting awake at every small noise, for hours. Then I heard a real sound—like the creak and moan of a tree scraping against a window, or an animal suffering in the night. I shivered nervously.

In a shaft of moonlight, I saw a figure step from behind a pile of potato sacks, and my fear fled. It was Aurelia. She peered through the dimness of the pantry and whispered, "Is that you, Zita?"

"Yes, of course it is. How ever did you get here? Didn't the guard in the hallway stop you, or was he sleeping at his job?"

Aurelia laughed. "No, he wasn't sleeping. I didn't come through the hallway. Look, I'll show you," and she pulled me into the pantry, shoved aside the bags of potatoes, and pointed out the hidden dumbwaiter.

I was thrilled. "Can I go up with you? Oh, please, can I? Can I sleep up there with you?"

"Of course you can come visit. We have all decided it. But I don't think you'd better stay. What if Cook discovered you were missing?"

"I'll wake early," I assured her. "I'll get back to my own bed before anyone knows. Oh, please!"

Aurelia gave in quickly. "Come on, then," she said. "And bring the pie left over from dinner!"

"Cook will be furious if I do," I said. "There's some leftover quince tart in the icebox. She'll never miss that." I pulled out the tart, ran back to the pantry, and climbed into the dumbwaiter with Aurelia, making sure to replace the potato sacks. It was a snug fit with both of us, but I loved to be so close to my sister. Aurelia gave a quick yank on one of the ropes, and slowly we began to ascend. We passed a door on the second floor, a door on the third floor, and then stopped at an open door, through which I could see the faces of Asenka and Anisa peering out at us.

"Zita! You're here!" Asenka said. The other girls crowded around me, chattering like sparrows. We saw each other so seldom that any meeting was a special treat for me, and I realized now that they too felt the bond that joins sisters together.

I was in their midst, and it was like heaven. They all wanted to brush my mop of red curls and admire my green eyes, so unlike theirs. When I asked if I could stay, they all said, "Of course you must stay!" in a single voice, then set to arguing about whom I would sleep with.

Aurelia stopped the discussion in her imperious way. "I'm the oldest, so she will sleep with me," she proclaimed. "Next time, she can sleep with you, Alanna, and the next time after that with Ariadne. We'll take turns in order of age."

"Why does Alanna get her before me? We're the same age!" complained Ariadne.

"You were born four minutes later," Aurelia reminded her. "Don't worry, you'll have your turn. Now," she said to me, "Nurse comes in to check us at midnight exactly, so you must hide under the bed till then. When she leaves, you can climb up with me. And you, Anisa, you must be the one who wakes Zita early, so she can get back downstairs without getting caught."

Anisa was pleased with her assignment and assured us all that she wouldn't sleep late. I crept under Aurelia's bed, as it was near midnight, and lay there without moving as Nurse walked through the room between the beds, checking to be sure each girl was sleeping soundly. I had to bite my cheeks to keep from giggling as I heard the various breathy sighs and snores my sisters put forth to convince Nurse they were deeply asleep. As soon as the door clicked behind her, I sprang out, brushing dust from my hair, and clambered into Aurelia's bed. It was heavenly; the feather mattress lofty and soft, the bedding silky smooth and scented with lavender. As Aurelia sang quietly to me, I dropped off to sleep and dreamed of the ballroom, alive again with dancers, swaying and stepping to the song my beautiful sister sang.

Just before dawn, as the first rooster crowed, Anisa shook me awake gently. She led me, stumbling with sleep, into the dumbwaiter and lowered me down to the pantry. By the time I reached the bottom I was awake, and I carefully replaced the potato sacks to be sure our secret would stay safe. I crept into my bed in the servants' quarters, tiptoeing to be sure not to wake the maids who shared my space, and crawled onto my rough mattress to snatch another few moments of sleep before the chores of the day began.

Chapter 3

In Which I Get to Know My Sisters

couldn't spend every night with the princesses, of course. We would have been found out, or expired from lack of sleep. I limited myself to one night a week, Sunday night, when the castle darkened early and people slept off the revels of their weekend trips into the nearby town.

All week I waited for Sunday night. I submitted meekly to my morning bath, knowing that in the evening my sisters would admire my clean hair and rosy skin, scrubbed with Cook's rough soap. I sat quietly through prayers, sneaking a look upward through my clasped hands to where my sisters sat in the chapel mezzanine. They looked like angels up there to me; sometimes a shaft of sunlight would pierce the stained-glass window high on the wall above them and scatter vivid blues and reds and golds over them. I helped without complaining as Cook prepared Sunday dinner, always a heavy, many-coursed repast that would have Cook sweaty and grumbling by the time the pudding was made. Sometimes the Sunday hours moved so slowly that I would swear every clock in the castle was broken, but at last nine o'clock would chime, and we would all head to our beds.

After the first few visits, I moved my nightly sleeping quarters to a tiny room at the end of the hallway— no more than a closet, really. But it was private, and I didn't have to worry about disturbing the three maids when I crept out to the dumbwaiter or back in at dawn. Cook narrowed her eyes at me when I told her I was moving, but I explained that Salina, the upstairs maid, had complained of my snoring, and I didn't like to think that I was keeping the others awake.

"Snoring!" Cook said. "A dose of castor oil might help that."

"Oh no," I protested. "It's the damp. Everyone snores—even you snore!"

This offended Cook and took her mind off castor

oil and off me. "Well, I never," she said, rolling out the dough for dumplings so fiercely that I was sure she imagined me under her rolling pin, flattened into compliance. "Me, snore? I sleep as quiet as a baby, I'll have you know."

"No, you're right," I backtracked quickly. "It's not you I was thinking of. It's Chiara. She snores terribly!" Chiara and Cook were often at war over the dispensation of keys to the pantries or the problem of dust from the flour bins. So Cook liked this.

"Like a lion roaring!" Cook agreed, chuckling, and no more was said of my new sleeping quarters.

Each Sunday night I crept down to the kitchen and into the dumbwaiter, usually clutching pieces of pie and tart that I had managed to hide away during the week, and tugged on the ropes as a signal. My sisters would haul on the ropes as I rose upward, past the staterooms, dark and silent, and then past the servants' quarters, where I could hear giggling or snores as the dumbwaiter creaked on its journey. At last I would arrive in the closet of my sisters' room, and they would pull me out of my cramped elevator, laughing and hugging me, and the fun would begin.

Some nights, my sisters would read to me or tell me stories they made up or had heard themselves. Alanna loved to read, especially stories about other princesses, and I learned the stories about Snow White and Rose Red, and Sleeping Beauty, and the terrible twisted dwarf Rumpelstiltskin, who tortured the queen to get her firstborn child. I especially loved Rapunzel, with her golden hair that I imagined was like Aurelia's, long and shining and straight. The tale of Beauty and her Beast, though, bewildered me. "Why did she go to the Beast?" I asked Alanna.

"To save her father," Alanna replied, showing me the illustration. In it, Beauty hugged her father as the Beast loomed over them both. "They love each other."

A father who loved his daughter . . . a daughter who loved her father. I could not understand this. Alanna, seeing my distress, put that story away, and we never read it again.

One Sunday night, Alima, the most musical of my sisters, decided I should learn to sing. All my sisters could play and sing to some extent, but Alima was brilliant on the lute and the pianoforte, and her voice was as clear and lovely as I imagined an angel's would be. The lesson was a disaster. I couldn't sing at all—I sounded like a frog in distress when I tried. My sisters collapsed in laughter, and though I was a little hurt, I could not help joining in.

"We shall teach you to dance instead!" Asenka pledged. Dancing was Asenka's specialty. The princesses paired off and showed me the popular dances—the allemande, and the gavotte, and the lavolta and ländler. They took turns squiring me up and down the room, and winced only a little when I trod on their feet or stumbled so that they barked their shins on the bed frames. Then Asenka danced the zambra for us, and we sat hypnotized by the swaying and twisting of her graceful body with its fall of silver hair.

A few weeks later Aurelia decided that I, like my sisters, must have pierced ears.

"She *is* a princess, really," she said, "and all princesses have pierced ears. That way, she can wear our earrings."

"You mean . . . you want to put holes in my ears?" I asked fearfully.

"I'll do it with a needle. It doesn't hurt," Aurelia said. "Look, I've had them since I was a baby. We all have." She pulled back her hair and showed me the sapphire drops that hung from her delicate ears.

"Well, if you got them when you were a baby, you don't remember whether it hurt, do you? It probably hurt horribly!" I was torn. I wanted to be like my sisters . . . but I didn't want them to stick needles through my ears.

Althea, looking worried, said, "We have to be sure her ears don't get infected. Hold the needle over the candle flame." Aurelia produced a long, evil-looking needle and held it over the flame until it grew so hot that she dropped it.

"There," she said, picking it up and blowing on it. "Come here, Zita."

Nervously, I came to her.

"Are you ready?" she asked. I nodded and closed my eyes. A moment later I felt a searing pain and screamed aloud, unable to help myself.

"Hush!" Aurelia cried. "Do you want Nurse to come in and find you?" Tears filled my eyes, but I shook my head fiercely.

"Do the other ear," I whispered. I was rewarded by a look of respect from Aurelia, and she quickly pierced the other ear and threaded small gold hoops through both.

"Clean them every day," Althea told me as the others crowded around me, admiring the earrings and wiping the tears from my face. "And be sure no one sees them!"

Aurelia pulled my hair back from my face so she could see the earrings. "They look so elegant," she said proudly. "Now you're a real princess, just like us."

I was a real princess only until Monday dawned, of course. Mondays were terrible for me that spring and summer. Sunday night was over, and for another whole week I was consigned to be a servant, watching my sisters from afar and longing to be with them. We waved to each other as we passed in hallways or on the land bridge, and sometimes they would pass me notes in clever ways. Once I found a piece of paper folded in the remains of a meat pie as I cleared the table. It was from Althea, the most kindhearted of my sisters, and read,

> *Dearest Zita,*
> *We have missed you this week. You looked especially forlorn during dinner last night, and we wanted you to know that we too are forlorn and longing to see you again on Sunday.*
>
> > *Your loving sister,*
> > *Althea*

A message like that could make me happy for days, and my sisters saw the results and tried to lift my spirits with little notes and gifts as often as they dared. I lived from Sunday to Sunday.

In July we were discovered. It was late in the evening, and Nurse had made her rounds. We had settled in to sleep—it was my night with Adena, one of my favorite bedmates. She was very slender, for one thing, so the two of us could fit easily into a bed made only for one, and her bedding was always scented with sandalwood, which gave me wonderful dreams. I had fallen into a lovely dream of a snow-white horse that I rode through a meadow, when the sudden jerk of Adena's body beside me woke me. Standing over the bed stood Nurse, and my sleep-glazed eyes saw her in a way I never had before. Her familiar face looked just the same, wrinkled as an old apple and just as sweet, and her hair was in her nighttime braids, which hung down to her waist in gray ropes. But her eyes were dark and sharp, the eyes of a much younger woman, and the way they looked at me frightened me. I whimpered and turned my head from her piercing stare, but when I looked back, she was the old Nurse with her kindly, brown-eyed gaze, and she smiled at me indulgently.

"I came back to find the comb I left behind, and look what I find instead. So little Zita is with her sisters!" she said, holding the candle so it wouldn't drip on me. She laughed at the sight of me, and my sisters laughed nervously with her.

"You won't tell, will you, Nurse?" wheedled Allegra. "It's just on Sundays, and we do love her so! It isn't fair that Father won't let her be with us."

Nurse pursed her lips. "No, dearies, it isn't fair at all. I think it's just lovely that you're all together like this. I won't tell, my pets—but you must be discreet. Don't let anyone know!"

We all shook our heads seriously. This would make

our Sundays so much easier—no more hiding from Nurse at the nightly checks, and no need to worry if she intercepted a smile or wave that passed between us, or even a note. I breathed a sigh of relief that Nurse hadn't been angry, ignoring the look she had given me at first. I'd been half asleep—perhaps it had even been part of my dream.

Nurse gave us each a nighttime drink of chocolate, and we gulped it down and laid our heads on the feather pillows. Then she tucked us in—even me, and I thrilled to the feel of her hands smoothing the quilt above me, just as if I were a real princess.

"Good night, dearies," Nurse said, and we echoed, "Good night!" back in unison. As the door closed, Adena hugged me.

"I was afraid she'd be mad," she whispered. "I thought she might make you go—or tell Father!"

I shivered at the thought. We all feared our father for his unpredictability and sudden rages, but my fear was different from my sisters'. They knew that he loved them, in his way. I had seen him gaze proudly at them as they rode with unusual grace or spoke a French phrase with perfect inflection. I had heard him gruffly compliment them when they looked especially lovely, with their hair in a becoming style or wearing a newly made dress.

I knew that other fathers loved their daughters as well. The maids Salina, Bethea, and Dagman often told tales of their fathers, men strong enough to swing young children onto their shoulders, protective enough to threaten a drunken suitor, loving enough to scratch out a dowry to ensure a good marriage. But my father turned away when he saw me, a scowl twisting his face. Despite what Cook had said to the contrary, I thought that he hated me and blamed me for my mother's death. It made me ache inside.

In my desire to please Father, I learned to bake. He loved sweets, and when he bit into a honey cake I had made one evening, his mouth pulled into the closest thing to a smile that he could manage.

"Cook!" he roared, sending the serving girls scurrying to the kitchen. I watched from behind the door as Cook rushed into the dining room, dipping low in an awkward curtsy and wiping her hands surreptitiously on her floury apron.

"Your Majesty," she managed. I laughed to myself to see her unnerved.

"This cake . . . ," Father said, gesturing with his fork. "It is unusually good."

Cook reddened with pleasure, but then she remembered who had actually made it. I could see the battle taking place within her as she tried to decide whether to tell. But her heart was big and true, and she sighed and said, "It was Zita's recipe, and her making."

The silence was immediate as my sisters, their tutor, and several of Father's councilors who sat at the long table stared down at their plates, pretending sudden fascination with the leftovers from their meal. Father deliberately took another bite, chewed slowly, and swallowed.

"Tell Zita it is very fine," he said finally, wiping his mouth with his linen napkin.

I clasped my hands together in glee as Cook curtsied again and backed from the room, almost falling over in her desire to be gone.

After that I experimented with tarts and pies, cakes and cookies, always trying to create a sweet that would bring that half smile again to Father's face. I watched from the doorway as he tasted each of my confections, and I imagined that his enjoyment was a compliment to me that he could not find the words to express.

On my twelfth birthday, which happily fell on a September Sunday, my sisters gave me an exquisite gift. It was a deep-green velvet coverlet for my bed. The silk embroidery, which they had done themselves, showed our own palace over the lake. The details were astonishing—a fish poked its head up from the silky blue water; a horseman clopped across the bridge;

willows bent low from the shore; and in a window high above the lake, a face showed. It was my face, surrounded by unmistakable red silk curls, smiling. The window was that of my sisters' bedroom.

"Oh, how beautiful!" I gasped, looking at the embroidered picture. "It's me in the window! I've never seen anything so wonderful!"

My sisters smiled proudly, and I peered more closely at my own face, tiny on the coverlet.

"What is that behind me?" I asked. There was a darkness there, behind the embroidered figure.

"Amina spilled some chocolate while we were working," Alanna said.

"I did not! That is just not so!" Amina protested. "The threads just . . . seem darker there. Nothing was spilled."

I looked again. It seemed there was a figure, nebulous and indistinct, behind me in the window.

"Maybe one of you pricked your finger, and it's blood," I suggested. "But it hardly shows. The embroidery is perfect. I shall use it every night." I hugged the coverlet to me, knowing that I would have to hide it beneath the rough blanket that covered my bed so that none of the servants would see it.

"Happy birthday, little Zita." Aurelia hugged me. "I remember when I turned twelve. It seems so long ago!"

Aurelia was as beautiful as ever, her hair as golden and lustrous, but a small line of discontent had begun to show sometimes between her eyes.

"When I was twelve . . . ," she began, and trailed off.

"What?" I urged, perching beside her on her bed and picking up her comb. I began to draw it gently through her long tresses, hoping for a story.

"When I was twelve, I thought everything would be different."

There was a sudden silence in the room, and I remembered that when Aurelia was twelve, our mother was still alive.

"Oh dear," Allegra whispered.

"I thought . . . ," Aurelia said. "I thought surely that by this age I would be married. I thought that I would have a husband, and perhaps a child. I thought that I would have a life so different from this one."

I stopped combing her hair and looked at her. Her lovely blue eyes were washed with tears, but she did not cry. I had never seen Aurelia cry.

"You *will* marry," Allegra said stoutly.

"Whom shall I marry? Since I have been of age, I have been unable to speak in the presence of any prince I have met. None of them would ever set foot in this place again. Who would marry a girl who does not speak? Or one with Father for a father? And who would marry a woman who will be queen, when he could not be king? Father has made it clear to me that he wants his blood to rule, and no one else's." Her voice was low and measured, and full of pain.

"Do you want to be queen?" I asked her.

"I am raised to be a queen," she told me fiercely. "It is all I know how to be. But I do not want to be queen all alone."

I couldn't bear to see her so unhappy, so I hugged her as hard as I could, feeling her stiff in my arms.

"I will find you a prince," I promised rashly. "I will find one who will rule with you as your consort."

Aurelia's eyes, which had been gazing far off into her unhappy future, came back to the present and focused on me. She smiled.

"All right," she said, and hugged me back. "You find me a consort, and I shall marry him. He and I will rule together, and I will raise you to your real stature. You will be a princess of the realm."

"And you my queen!" I laughed, and my sisters laughed with me, glad to see Aurelia herself again. We all prostrated ourselves before her, calling her "Your Highness" and "Your Majesty" and giggling wildly.

But this knowledge changed something in the way I saw my sisters. It wasn't just Aurelia who felt this way. Alanna, Ariadne, Althea, Adena, Asenka, Amina, and

Alima were all old enough to marry, and in any other kingdom would have wed long ago. They would have met princes from far and near, danced at balls at home and abroad, worn dresses that showed off their white shoulders and blue eyes. Instead, they were trapped in a pink palace whose walls sweated, with no husbands in sight. My other sisters would be marriageable soon, if they were not already, and I too would come of age before long. Whom would I marry? A footman, a stableman? The dreadful Burle? But I was a princess, not a servant!

For the next few days I was in a funk, confused and irritable. I'd spent my life envying my sisters, but now I was beginning to see that they were just as trapped in their lives as I was in mine. They were more comfortable, it is true, but they were prisoners nonetheless. What would become of us? Would we live out our lives in this palace, alone and unloved? Would we grow old here, our joints aching until our knees would no longer bend, childless and bereft? I had never thought much about a husband or family, but now that I suddenly realized I might not have them, they were becoming very important to me.

My mood was so bad that when Cook chastised me for inattention to the soup, I threw the ladle at her, spattering pea puree up the walls. Cook was furious, but she couldn't punish me as she would another maid, so she banished me from the kitchen's warmth and dryness and sent me over the land bridge to search for fallen nuts for a tart. It was an early fall morning, and on the lake surface leaves floated, their reds and oranges reflected in the leaves still hanging on the tree branches above. The air was crisp and clean, and I breathed deeply as I crossed the bridge, glad to be away from the palace.

At the edge of the woods I stopped and looked back— and saw something most unusual. My sisters were coming out of the palace for their afternoon stroll, and I watched them walk across the bridge, their bright cloaks billowing around them. They ambled slowly along the lakeshore, stopping now and then to pick up a bright leaf or blow the fluff from a dandelion as Nurse herded them like a flock of sheep. Then I saw their heads tilt up as one, and I looked into the distance to see what had caught their interest. I made out riders on horseback—three, four, no, five of them, riding slowly out of the forest on the far side of the bridge. They wore soldiers' uniforms, the sky blue and black of the men who patrolled the Western Reaches that ran through my father's kingdom and the neighboring kingdom of Blaire. I watched them approach, their leader a bearded soldier with auburn hair under his military cap who sat tall and straight in the saddle. I could see from the stripes on his sleeve that he was a captain. At first the soldiers did not seem to see the princesses, and then the captain pulled up sharply at the same time that Nurse noticed the riders.

"Princesses!" I heard Nurse's voice clearly through the cool air. "Come along—we must get back!" Scurrying like a sheepdog, she gathered my sisters together, protecting them and moving them back the way they had come. But Aurelia stayed where she was, her face raised in the brilliant fall sunlight. I saw her look straight at the auburn-haired captain, and he looked back at her. From my vantage point, I could not see their expressions, but I felt the stillness between them, and I raised my hand to my mouth to stifle a gasp. The captain bowed his head to Aurelia, and she dipped ever so slightly in a curtsy before Nurse descended on her.

"Princess Aurelia!" she scolded. "Do not curtsy to a soldier!"

Aurelia turned, and I could see the flush of embarrassment rising on her cheeks as she allowed Nurse to lead her back to join the others. I stood at the woods' edge, confused and transfixed by what I had witnessed, and the captain too held his mount still, watching as my sisters scurried back to the bridge. I could hear the other soldiers laughing and joking, but he just sat unmoving as the girls disappeared inside the palace. Then he turned his horse smartly and galloped back into the trees, the other four following behind.

I carried my basket far into the woods, thinking about the soldier and Aurelia, and picking up the occasional walnut and hazelnut along the way. At noontime, I sat beside a brook to eat my bread and cheese, and then I lay relishing the warmth of the autumn sun and looking up at the brilliant blue of the sky, a blue as clear as Akila's eyes. And I must have fallen asleep, for I dreamed a terrible dream.

A storm had come unexpected upon the palace, and my sisters were out in their boats, three pretty rowboats painted pastel yellow, green, and blue. The sky above the lake was black with clouds, and the lake was black too, its waters whipped into waves that lashed the sides of the boats as the girls clutched one another and shrieked in fear. As I watched in my dream, powerless to move, a great waterspout formed behind the boats, whirling and whirling the lake water upward, and one by one the boats were swept into it, splintering apart from the force of the spinning winds. I could do nothing but point wordlessly in horror as my sisters were drawn upward to their certain deaths. A moment after the boats had disappeared, the winds died, the waterspout disappeared, and the clouds parted, showing the sky as blue as blue could be. There was no sign of the storm, and no sign of my sisters. I began to scream and scream, and woke still screaming.

Darkness was coming on, and the clear sky had turned gray, with clouds spitting out a cold rain. I pulled my shawl around me and stood, still confused by my deep sleep and fearsome dream. I thought I heard shouts, and then realized there was indeed someone calling my name.

"Zita! Is that you? Are you all right?" It was a voice I did not recognize, nor did I recognize the boy who came crashing into my clearing a moment later.

"Was that you shouting?" he demanded. "Are you hurt?"

I rubbed my eyes, trying to focus. "Who are you?" I asked.

"Breckin. I'm the new stableboy. Cook sent me to look for you—she was getting worried."

"What kind of name is Breckin?" I said crossly, my head heavy with sleep.

He laughed. "It means 'freckled,'" he said. "I came out of the womb like this."

I looked at him. Freckled he was indeed—his face and hands, all I could see of his skin, were speckled with orange. It gave him a friendly look, somehow. I smiled at him.

"I fell asleep," I told him. "I had a bad dream, and I

think I must have yelled. But I'm fine."

"Well, you won't be for long if we don't get back!" Breckin said. "There's a storm coming on, and you know the wolves are out this time of year."

I had never seen a wolf, and knew no such thing, but the cold breeze made me shiver and I could see the wisdom in his words. I picked up my basket. Breckin tried to take it from me, but I kept a good hold on it.

"I can carry it!" I said. He shrugged.

"Doesn't look like you got much, anyway," he said. "Cook won't like that!"

I started back along the path through the trees. "I'm not afraid of Cook."

"Really?" Breckin drew even with me. "Why not? I hear she's got a quick hand with the switch! Everyone's afraid of her."

I snorted. "Cook's harmless. That switch just whistles through the air—it never actually hits anything. She's all talk. Besides, she wouldn't dare hit me."

Breckin raised an eyebrow. "She wouldn't dare? Why's that? Have you some special power over her? Are you a witch, perhaps?"

"Hush!" I said swiftly. I turned around in a circle and spat over my shoulder to ward off evil. "Don't say that—even in jest. Of course I'm not a witch. I'm a princess."

Breckin hooted, and suddenly I didn't think his freckles were so charming. "You're a princess, are you? Like one of the blond beauties upstairs? Well, pleased to meet you. I'm a knight in shining armor, myself." He bowed deeply to me, and I pulled a branch toward me and let it fly, smacking him on the head.

The branch left a red welt on his forehead, and in an instant he was after me. I ran as fast as I could along the darkening path, dodging vines and stumps, laughing and gasping as I fled. I was strong and quick, and Breckin did not catch me until we were nearly back at the lakeshore, where he grabbed my shoulders and spun me around and shook me. The nuts spilled out from my basket.

"You could've taken out my eye!" he said.

"Ah, but I missed," I retorted. "Instead, I've just erased a few of your freckles."

For a minute I thought he really was angry, but then he burst out laughing, and I realized that I liked this Breckin very much indeed. I put my hand up to the welt on his forehead and touched it gently.

"I am sorry," I said. "Come into the kitchen and I'll find some salve to put on it. Cook keeps some for burns, but it works on scrapes and cuts as well."

We gathered the nuts as well as we could in the dim

light and made our way over the land bridge and into the kitchen. I managed to dress Breckin's wound before Cook saw me, and he hurried back to his duties in the stables. But before he left, we agreed to meet again in secret. We would both finish our tasks with all speed the next day, and in the late afternoon, if we could get away, he would take me riding. I was so pleased with this plan that I did not mind Cook's wrath when she saw that I had collected barely enough nuts for a single tart, much less the five she'd made crusts for, and I smiled to myself as I shelled the nuts and then peeled apple after apple to fill the four remaining crusts.

Chapter 4

In Which I Meet a Witch

o longer did my life revolve around Sunday nights with my sisters. Now when Monday dawned, I knew I might see Breckin. The weeks sped by, and I spent more and more time outside, though the weather grew cold and ice formed in the shallows of the lake. Breckin taught me to ride a horse, and I was pleased to find that I was very good at it. "Better than your sisters," he told me, having realized that I'd been telling the truth when I told him I was a princess. He'd heard the whole story from the horse master and thought it was appalling. "You can't blame a child for its mother's death!" he protested about my father's treatment of me, but when I just shrugged he left it alone. He was good to talk to, always ready with a jest but able to be quiet, too.

We walked in companionable silence through the forest one morning. It was a warm day, with the muted sunshine that comes only after the first frost, giving a clarity to the yellowed fields and vivid trees. Our feet scuffed aside brilliant fallen leaves as we searched for signs of truffles under the earth. Father loved them shaved on scrambled eggs, and they only grew at the base of certain oaks, and then only at certain times and under certain conditions. We had once had a pig that could sniff them out, but she got loose one day, dug up and ate every truffle that existed for miles around, and then took herself off to a neighboring kingdom to eat theirs. Only recently had the truffles repopulated, but I was terrible at finding them. We had yet to see if Breckin could do better.

I had learned much about Breckin during the past weeks. We had shared our likes and dislikes: he did not like eating things that were green, or wearing wool, which made him itch; he loved nuts of all kinds. I told him that I could take nuts or leave them, but chocolate— that was my passion. He admitted that he feared snakes above all things, and I told him of my uncanny fear of rats. I admitted to him that even the water rats that sometimes swam along the edges of the lake spooked me, though I knew they weren't real rats.

Breckin came from the kingdom of Blaire to the west, where King Tobin ruled. He'd been raised on a farm deep in the country with a brother and sister, and when his father died, his mother had turned to bees.

"Bees?" I asked. "What does she do with bees?"

"She keeps them and harvests their honey, of course," Breckin said.

I was astonished. We did not keep bees, and it had never occurred to me to wonder where our honey came from. Cook bought it at market, and it arrived in green-tinted glass jars to keep the sun from spoiling it. I had thought—well, I had not thought at all. Perhaps I had assumed that honey was distilled from a plant or was mined from the hills. All I knew was that it sweetened cakes wonderfully.

"Bees," I repeated, amazed. Breckin laughed at my ignorance, but it was a kind laugh.

I learned that his sister was wed, and that she and her husband helped with the honey business. His brother was a soldier, guarding the Western Reaches, and Breckin missed him very much. I found it all fascinating—the lives of ordinary folk.

"Was it very different, where you lived?"

He laughed. "Well, of course it was. It was a farm

beside a tiny village, not a palace built over a lake. We'd no royalty there—the only king was our banty rooster." He was quiet for a minute, and then said, "There was another difference, too. A difference in the air, or something. Your kingdom has such a strange feel to it."

"What do you mean, a strange feel?" I asked.

"It's hard to explain. When you come over the border from Blaire at Mickle Crossing, there's a difference. It's like . . . oh, I don't know, exactly. Like a sort of silence. A lack of something."

"Ah," I said, nodding. "That's the lack of magic."

He stared at me. "You have no magic at all here?"

"Father forbade it, when Aurelia was born. He didn't want a curse on any of his children. He sent all the witches and wizards out of the kingdom, big and small. We don't even have a soothsayer." I regretted this very much, for I thought it would be interesting to know the future.

"Ah! That's why it's so damp and all," Breckin said.

Of course it was. I'd never thought of it before, but surely any decent witch or wizard could dry up damp. I shook my head. "How stupid!" I said. "Think of all the things gone moldy that didn't have to!"

"It must have been very odd, living with no magic," Breckin mused.

"Why, did you have a lot of it where you grew up?"

He smiled, remembering. "We had a neighbor who was a healing witch. It's a great thing to live near one of those. We were never ill. Nobody in our village ever died of sickness, hardly. Or even of accidents, unless they were really terrible ones. She could heal bone breaks and cuts. When my brother and I were little, whenever we'd fall down—or hit each other—and we'd be bleeding and crying, Mother would send us over to Elba's house to get fixed."

I stopped walking. "How did she fix you?"

"She'd give us a cup of chocolate, and then wash the cut or scrape. Then she'd put something on it—it smelled vile and stung. But a few minutes later—nothing! As if the cut had never happened. No scar at all."

I thought about this. I'd gotten my share of cuts and burns working around the knives and fires of the kitchen. My hands were marked all over from accidents, and I always felt vaguely ashamed of them on Sundays with my sisters, comparing my red, scarred skin to their porcelain hands.

"I wonder if she can fix scars after they've set," I mused, and we walked on.

A little later, I wondered aloud, "Then how did your father die, if there were no accidents or sicknesses in your village?"

Breckin was silent, and I was afraid I'd offended or hurt him by asking. Then he said, "He fell off a roof that he was fixing. He was killed right away. There was no chance for him to be healed."

"Oh, I am sorry!" I said. "I hope you don't mind that I asked." I snuck a look at him to see if he was upset or angry, but he just looked as he always did.

"It's all right," he replied. "It was a long time ago. I was only four. I barely remember him."

We had that in common, Breckin and I, both losing a parent before we were old enough to have memories of them. I wondered, though, if Breckin missed his father as I missed my mother—missing the idea of her because I had not known the real person to miss.

Then I saw an oak tree with a peculiar bare patch at its base. "There!" I said, pointing. Gingerly, with sticks, we dug down to the tree's roots and found a rough round ball that smelled of mold and rot and a little like mushrooms, "with a touch of sweaty feet," Breckin said, sniffing it and grimacing. "People eat these?"

"Just a tiny little bit at a time. It's like an herb," I told him. "A great delicacy."

"They can have them!" he said. We wrapped the truffle and placed it in a sack Breckin carried and then walked on, looking for a place to stop and eat the lunch that Cook had packed. I'd added to it liberally, as Cook didn't know that I would not be hunting truffles alone, and we sat under a willow on the edge of a brook and ate cold fowl and cheese, bread and pears, and drank from the sparkling stream.

After lunch, we lay back for a while and watched the white clouds scud across the sky, but the breeze was chilly, so before long we rose again and walked on, still searching for the elusive truffles. We were now in a part of the forest I did not know. Though I wasn't afraid of much, the woods at nightfall did have a place in my nightmares, so I would not have gone so far by myself. Here the trees arched overhead so I couldn't see the sky. The gloom they cast made me shiver, and if I had been alone, I would have turned back and walked very quickly home. With Breckin, though, it was an adventure, and I was pleased to follow the stream up to a little waterfall that plashed on the rocks below. We dug up another truffle a bit farther on, and then I saw something between the trees that caught my eye.

"Look!" I said to Breckin, pulling at his arm. There, deeply shaded by tall fir trees, was a ruined cottage, its roof sagging, its walls crooked and leaning. It looked as if it had been deserted for a century. Brambles grew up around it, trying to push their way in at the door. The two windows in front gazed like blind eyes, crusted over with the dirt of decades.

We walked hesitantly up the remains of the front path and pushed aside vines to peer in at one of the windows. The cracked glass was filthy, and we could see nothing.

"Let's go in," Breckin suggested. I was horrified.

"There are probably rats in there!" I protested. "And the roof could fall in on us at any moment!"

"Oh, don't be such a—" He broke off. I could always tell when he remembered that I was a princess. He would stop whatever rude thing he was saying or doing and give me a look that I couldn't interpret. And then he would grin and go on as before.

"Well, I'm going in," he said, grinning that grin. He pushed at the front door, and to our astonishment it swung open smoothly. He stepped inside, and I crowded behind him. My jaw dropped open as I peered around.

The inside of the cottage was not ruined at all. In fact, it was clean and pretty and bright, with knotted rugs on wide-beamed floors, a cheery fire burning in the fireplace, chairs with plump cushions, and ruffled curtains at the windows. The smell of shortbread scented the air, and a teakettle began to whistle as I started to back away.

"Let's go!" I whispered. "This is too peculiar. Come on, Breckin!"

"Wait—," he started, and then we heard a door

unlatch. We could see, from our position at the front of the house, the door at the back of the house as it opened, and my heart leaped into my throat as we watched to see who would enter. I felt a great wave of relief as I saw an old woman, tiny and bent with age, come in with an armful of fall flowers—chrysanthemums and late daisies. She smiled when she saw us standing there, not at all surprised or concerned that we had come into her house without so much as a knock.

"Come in, children!" she said. "Come and have some tea and cookies."

"B-beg pardon, ma'am," Breckin stammered. "We thought—it seemed like the place was deserted. We never would have . . ."

The old woman laughed so heartily that neither of us could help smiling. "I can still do a good illusion, if I do say so!" she said.

"Illusion?" Breckin said. "Are you a witch, then?"

"Breckin!" I chided him. In my father's home, to be called a witch was to be insulted.

"That's all right, my dear," the woman said calmly. "I am indeed a witch." I gasped in shock as, moving spryly for someone her age, she placed the flowers in a pitcher and filled it with water from a jug. "Do sit down. Would you like some tea?"

Breckin and I looked at each other. He was very

excited, I could tell, but all I could think was *What if Father finds out?*

"You don't need to worry, dear," the old woman said to me. I looked at her, confused. Had I spoken aloud? "Your father's never noticed me yet, and I've been living here a long, long time. I've made the place seem deserted, you see, and I can always tell who is coming. I'm in no danger of being found out, and neither are you."

I was astounded. She knew who I was and who my father was. She had known we were coming! She was a soothsayer at least—maybe more. I slipped past Breckin and moved farther into the house. Cautiously I took a seat at the wooden table in the kitchen. Breckin followed me and sat too. The witch poured steaming water into a little pot from which a lovely raspberry smell rose. Then she opened the cast-iron door of the stove and pulled out a pan. Ah—the source of the shortbread aroma! I did love shortbread.

She cut the shortbread into pieces and put the pieces onto a chipped plate, poured the tea into mismatched cups, placed a bowl of sugar on the table, and brought tea and cookies over to us as we sat watching. Her movements were so smooth and graceful that we did not think to ask if we could help her; indeed, I wondered whether perhaps her aged appearance was another of her illusions. Again she appeared to read my mind and laughed merrily. "I'm quite as old as I look, dear. Maybe even older!"

We spent a few lovely minutes eating warm, silky shortbread and sipping our tea. I thought that I had never eaten anything so sweet and delicious, nor ever tasted tea so much like real raspberries before. I caught Breckin's eye and saw that he felt the same, and we smiled at each other.

"Now," the old woman said when we paused in our eating and drinking. "You must tell me a little about yourselves, my dears. I could see your coming, but not why. Do you have a trouble that needs attention? You, Zita, are you plagued by your father and his temper?"

I choked on my cookie and coughed, and Breckin pounded me on the back. "Stop!" I said crossly to him, and to the old woman, "How did you know my name?"

She smiled sweetly at me, and I marveled to see how much she looked like I'd imagined a witch would. Her nose was sharp and pointed and came close to meeting her sharp and pointed chin. Her eyes were a lively, sparkling black, and her white hair curled about her wrinkled cheeks like sheep's wool.

"I am so unforgivably rude, my dears," she said. "We have not even introduced ourselves, have we? I am

Babette, which means, of course, 'enchanter.' And you, young man?"

"Breckin, ma'am, from the kingdom of Blaire," Breckin told her, reaching for another piece of shortbread. "I work in King Aricin's stables."

"Breckin is a fine name, for you are freckled indeed," she said. "But I can tell that your name does not tell the whole story. And you, my dear?"

"You already know my name," I said. "And you know where I'm from, and who my father is." My tone was more belligerent than I had meant it to be, and Breckin frowned at me. "Sorry," I added.

Babette laughed. "Don't be sorry," she said. "It's true. But that doesn't tell me who you are. You are Zita, but who is she?"

"The patron saint of servants," I muttered, embarrassed.

"Yes, that's so," Babette acknowledged. "The name has other meanings, too, did you know?"

"It does?" I had never heard this. All I knew was that I'd been named as a curse.

"Oh yes," Babette assured me. "*Zita* means 'little rose' as well. And it means 'seeker.'"

"Seeker," I repeated. "One who seeks? Seeks what?"

"That is what you will have to decide," Babette said. "It is a good name, an excellent name. Just right for you."

I thought about it as I chewed shortbread. I was pleased. It was much better to be a seeker than a servant. Exciting, even.

"Ma'am—Babette, ma'am," Breckin started, and I sprayed out crumbs as I giggled at his discomfort over calling her by name. He glared at me and continued, "Why are you still here, when witches are forbidden? Isn't it dangerous? Shouldn't you cross the border, go someplace you would be more welcome?"

"Why, child, I'm not in danger," Babette assured him. "They've stopped hunting witches long since. Even if they were looking, I've protected myself well. And this is my home, you know. I'd lived here a very long time when the king decided to forbid witchcraft. I couldn't leave, nor did I want to. Besides, I have work to do here."

"Work?" I asked, intrigued. "You mean witch work? Spells and the like?"

"It may come to that," she replied comfortably. "I don't know, exactly. I just know I'll be needed."

"By whom?" Breckin asked.

Babette smiled, her bright eyes nearly disappearing in the wrinkled creases of her face. "Well, we shall have to see, won't we? Maybe by you, my lad!" She laughed, and Breckin laughed with her, but I looked at her long and hard. Was she a good witch, or a bad one? The stories were full of bad witches, casting spells to turn people into this and that or enchant them into endless sleeps or poison them with perfect fruits. Who could say what kind of witch Babette was, appearing as she did out of nowhere, in her ruined cottage?

Again she seemed to read my mind. "You don't have to fear me, my love," she said reassuringly to me. "I will never do you any harm. I knew your mother, you see."

I gasped. "You knew her? When? How? Oh, please— tell me!"

"We met while she was gathering herbs one afternoon. She had just married your father. She loved to wander in the woods—like you, my dear. She was very like you."

"Like me?" I protested. "No! She was beautiful. She was . . . magical. How can you say she was like me?"

Babette laughed. "She was beautiful indeed. She had your sisters' lovely hair, their vivid eyes and pale skin. But she had your liveliness, your spirit. Before . . ."

"Before . . . ," I repeated.

"When she began to have children, and your father's disappointment and sadness began to crush her, that spirit disappeared. It was terrible to watch."

"Couldn't you have helped her?" I asked.

"After your father banished magic, she did not come to see me anymore. She wanted so much to please him—

it was her undoing. And I could not have helped her, even if she had come."

"Why not?" I demanded. "You're a witch. You could have worked magic to help her—to give her a son!"

"Witches shouldn't interfere with childbearing. That is a more powerful magic than any we work. There are very few of us who could have an effect on that—make a pregnancy give forth a girl or boy, make a woman fertile who is not. It is too strong a magic for us. It could only end badly. I longed to help her, but I could not." Babette sighed, and I echoed her inwardly. My eyes were filled with tears. My poor mother!

"Don't cry, child," Babette said softly. "I could not help her, but I can help you, if you should ever need it. You can always find me here."

"How can we find you?" Breckin asked. "It was only by accident that we came across your house—I don't think we could ever find it again."

Babette rose and went to the front window. "Look out," she said to us. We followed her and peered outside. We saw a tidy front yard, with fall flowers lining a straight walkway that led up to the front door.

"If you come into the woods and picture this path, it will be there. As long as you see it straight and true in your mind's eye, you will be able to walk it up to my door. Don't let the illusion confuse you. The house is here, as you see it now. The path is here. You will be here too, if you keep your mind focused and clear."

The shadows were long—it was getting late. I thought suddenly about Cook, waiting for our truffles. What would she do if we did not come home before dark? I could imagine soldiers and servants trampling through the woods, coming upon the cottage, shouldering their way inside. "We have to go!" I said, panicked.

"Yes," Babette agreed. "Go straight back. But come again. Come, if anything strange or frightening should happen. Or if you just want tea and cookies, come."

We took our leave of the witch, submitting to her warm hug. I breathed in deeply of the vanilla smell that rose from her clothing, and felt her soft hair against my cheek. It seemed a little like hugging my mother, hugging someone who had known her and loved her. I carried that feeling home with me, using it to ward off my fear of the dark underbrush and looming trees as we trekked through the forest. Night had fallen when we burst out of the woods in sight of the lake and the palace, and I said a quick good-bye to Breckin. He ran off to the stables, on the shore near the land bridge, and I sped over the bridge and into the kitchen to face the wrath of Cook.

Chapter 5

In Which a Change Takes Place

hat evening we were found out, and I was desolate. From an upstairs window, Chiara had seen me parting from Breckin and had told Cook. Cook was furious, and nothing I said could sway her.

"You cannot be gallivanting around with a stableboy! You are a princess, and if you don't care about your position, you are also a girl who is in my charge! The things that could happen . . ."

"What could happen?" I asked innocently, though in fact I was not quite so innocent. I'd seen the trysts that maids and footmen arranged and carried out in the darker corners of the palace. I'd seen the girls who left the palace weeping, pale and swollen, never to return—and the men who left jauntily, whistling gaily but unable to meet anyone's eyes. Cook was not distracted by my question, though.

"Never you mind, Zita! That's neither here nor there. You may not see that boy again, and if you do, he shall be dismissed. Do you hear me?" She waved her rolling pin threateningly.

"Oh, Cook," I pleaded. "He is my friend. I have so little fun, except when I am with him. Please don't make us stop." I bent my head in supplication, but looked up from under my lashes to see the effect of my words.

True to form, Cook was moved, and I could see her frown and shake her head. "Poor child," she said. "But I cannot allow it. What if your father knew? He'd have me out of here before you could say 'pie.' And where would I go?"

"Father? Why would he care?" I was startled by her words.

"Oh, he keeps an eye on you," Cook informed me. "Every so often he asks. Other times I see him watching you."

I was both intrigued and unnerved by the idea of Father watching me. I spent a great deal of my time avoiding him—hiding in broom closets or behind statuary in the hallway as he passed, dashing down the stairs if I heard him above me, sending others to do work in rooms where I thought he might be. I knew I could not expect his appreciation of my baking to affect his feelings for me much, so I thought it best to keep out of his way. I was used to believing that he did not notice me. But perhaps Cook told the truth. Perhaps he thought of me, wondered what I was doing, watched me. If Cook was right about that, though, then she was right about Breckin. I could not see him again without endangering his position. Father would surely let him go if we were seen together.

"All right, Cook," I said unhappily. "But can I let him know, so he doesn't seek me out? Can I send him a note?"

Cook was aghast. "A note! Put words on paper addressed to a stableboy? And what if someone else sees that note? Child, what are you thinking? I'll tell him myself, don't you worry. He won't go looking for you, you can be sure."

I could imagine just what Cook might say to Breckin, and I apologized to him for it in my mind. But there was nothing I could do.

It was several days before my path and Breckin's crossed again. I was sent to gather eggs in the henhouse, a job I despised. I thought chickens were the stupidest creatures on earth, always panicking over nothing, or sitting still when real danger threatened. Often I entered the henhouse to find birds lying headless and covered in blood, victims of a weasel or fox they'd been too dim-witted to call out against. When I lifted the hens to remove the eggs from beneath them, they pecked at me, leaving marks on my hands and arms, and I longed to wring their necks. I didn't even like eating chicken, for remembering their beady eyes and idiotic cackling.

Breckin was taking Allegra's horse, Bounty, back to the stables after she'd ridden her out, and we walked in parallel for a moment.

"I'm sorry we can't meet," he said in a low voice, not looking at me. Anyone who peered at us from the palace windows would see us just walking near each other, not communicating in any way.

"I hope Cook did not take a rolling pin to you," I said, trying not to move my mouth too much. He snorted with suppressed laughter.

"My ears were blistered, but my backside was spared," he said, and I blushed. "Listen, Zita, why don't we meet at the witch's house? Next Saturday, at noon if you can?"

"If I can," I said, delighted, and veered away to the henhouse. This time, when the hens clucked and pecked, I was so happy that I playfully clucked back at them and moved my head as if to peck as well. Startled, they fluttered their wings and jumped off the nests, and I picked out the eggs more easily than usual.

That Sunday night I found myself in the unusual position of having to keep a secret from my sisters. I never had done so before, partly because I knew no secrets of consequence, and partly because any little secrets I did know—which maid loved which servant, whether the underbutler and Chiara were feuding—I presented to my sisters as the price of entry to their bedchamber. They loved to hear my little scandals, sequestered as they were by their position as royal princesses. Nothing ever happened to them, they complained, and so they were thrilled to hear about lovers' triangles and arguments and petty thefts. And when I had met Breckin and got to know him, I'd told them all. In fact, my stories of my rambles with the stableboy were the highlight of the evening, most Sundays, my sisters hanging breathlessly on my descriptions of our treks through the forest and our conversations. But I did not tell them about the witch. I felt guilty, keeping such a big and juicy secret. Still, it was my very own to keep. I did not wish to share it with anyone.

My sisters gathered around to hear about my outing with Breckin for truffles, but I left out the discovery of the cottage and what was inside. To make up for my secrecy, I repeated as much of our discussions as I could recall, and they listened avidly. As I described the way Breckin's funny freckles danced on his face when he smiled, I heard a sigh and saw Asmita looking dreamily at the fire.

"Do you think he will kiss you?" she asked.

I was shocked. "Kiss me! I should think not!" In fact, it had never dawned on me that he might. It was a very peculiar thought and made me feel quite warm and uncomfortable.

"Of course he will kiss you," Aurelia said. Her voice was low and unhappy. "You will be kissed before I ever am, though you are not even half my age."

I jumped down off Anisa's bed and ran to Aurelia, where she sat on the edge of her mattress. "I won't do it, I promise," I said to her earnestly, holding both her hands in mine. "You shall be kissed first of all of us. It's only fair!"

Aurelia smiled at me, but the little crease between her eyebrows remained, and I realized that it was there all the time now. I reached up to smooth it with my fingers but caught myself and pulled back. I looked at my other older sisters—Alanna, Ariadne, Althea—and I could see a worry and a discontent on each of their brows. They had been waiting for so long. I shook my head, angry all at once at my poor sisters' fate. I meant what I said. I would not be kissed first. If they could not, I would not.

At the end of that week, my father tried once more to introduce suitors to his daughters. We all watched at a third-floor window as the princes Bazyli and Ade, brothers from Tem, rode up to the palace on very fine steeds, though the princes themselves were, my sisters felt, of the second tier. Bazyli was rather plump—"But he has a kind face!" Althea was quick to point out. And Ade's complexion was quite bad. We all tried to think of something nice to say about his pockmarked cheeks, but the best we could do was Anisa's "Well, he must have been very brave, suffering through the pox."

The five eldest girls—Adena was now permitted to attend—were to dine with the princes. "You must speak!" I urged them, adjusting their trains and straightening their tiaras. "Don't be shy."

"It isn't shyness," Althea said disconsolately. "It's just—I don't know. When they talk to me, I feel that my tongue will not work. It almost seems to swell in my mouth and keep the words from coming. I want to speak, but I just cannot."

"Nor I," said Alanna. "But I will surely try!"

They kissed me and hurried down the stairs to the princes. The other princesses and I watched from the upper stair as Father introduced Bazyli and Ade. My sisters dipped in their most graceful curtsies, extending their hands, but they did not speak, and still silent, they went in to dinner.

Afterward, Cook and I, and Nurse, who had come to get the evening chocolate, were in the kitchen, and we could not help overhearing Father's fury as he stormed up and down the hallway above us.

"*Why* do you not speak?" he shouted. "Were the princes not to your liking? Have you so many suitors that you can offend all who come here?"

"I am sorry, Father," I heard Aurelia say sadly. "Truly, I wanted to talk. But everything I thought to say seemed so silly—I could not get the words out."

"You are spoiled, every one of you!" Father roared. "I have indulged you overmuch. Too many dresses, too much finery. What need have you of tutors or dance masters—or a nurse, for that matter? You are too old for a nurse! You are spinsters now, not children. I will dismiss them all!"

I stole a glance at Nurse, who had gone very pale.

"Father, no!" Althea cried. "We will do better next time—I promise you!"

"Next time? There will be no next time. No prince will court the mute daughters of Aricin. You are a humiliation to me. Get out of my sight!" There was a flurry of slippers on stairs and the sound of stifled sobs as they rushed to their room, and then a great quiet descended. Cook pursed her lips.

"Well," she said, "those princes were not worthy, and our princesses knew it. I would not have spoken either!"

I laughed, but uncomfortably, as I handed Nurse the tray with its pot of chocolate and cups.

"He means nothing by it, Nurse," I said, trying to comfort her. "I am sure he won't dismiss you. He is just angry. He'll get over it."

Nurse shook her head. "Poor poppets," she murmured. "I must tend to them," and she hurried off upstairs.

When I walked into the forest the next morning for my meeting with Breckin at Babette's cottage, I was trying very hard not to think about the conversation I'd had with my sisters about kisses and kissing. It was difficult. Every time I did think of it, I became a little breathless, and I could feel how I flushed. If I should do that in front of Breckin, surely he would know what I was thinking. I would be humiliated. I would die.

Instead I tried to focus my attention on the path through the wood. At first I remembered just how Breckin and I had gone, but as the trees came thicker and closer, they began to look all alike. In no time I was completely lost.

I sat on a fallen log and tried to think. There had

been a stream, I recalled, and a waterfall. A big oak tree—or was that on the way back? Then I remembered the witch's words to us: *If you come into the woods and picture this path, it will be there. As long as you see it straight and true in your mind's eye, you will be able to walk it up to my door.* I strained, trying to imagine the path to the cottage. There—I could almost see it. Pretty white stones, edged with chrysanthemums, orange and yellow. I thought of it as hard as I could, then stood and began to walk forward. Under my feet I felt the soft carpet of pine needles, heard the crackle of the fall leaves, and then I felt the *crunch, crunch* of pebbles. Startled, I looked up. There was the cottage, trim and tidy, its window boxes overflowing with flowers, even in this cold autumn season.

I gave a shout of triumph and ran forward, up the stairs to the door. There was a knocker on it that hadn't been on the ruined door we'd seen the other time. I looked closely at it. It was carved in the shape of a frog, so cleverly that it almost looked alive. As I thought this, the frog extended one long leg and gave a smart rap at the door. I screamed in shock and stumbled backward, fell down the front steps onto the gravel path. As I sat picking gravel out of my palms, feeling extremely foolish, the front door opened and Babette looked out.

"Oh, my dear, whatever happened?" she cried worriedly. "Are you all right?"

I blushed. "I'm fine," I said. "It was the knocker—it startled me."

She frowned at the frog on the door, and it stuck its long tongue out at her. "You should be more careful," she scolded it. "And more respectful!" Its tongue flicked out again, and I started to laugh.

"Is that an illusion too?" I asked, standing and brushing myself off.

"No, that's an enchantment. It's a real frog, turned into a door knocker. It hopped into my house when it rained the other night, so instead of putting it back out, I just—well, you see."

"Poor thing," I said, forgiving it for scaring me.

Babette gave me a look. "I suppose so," she said thoughtfully. "I'm sure it would rather be on the bank of a pond somewhere. I'll let it go." She murmured some words, and the frog, green now instead of wood brown, dropped to the top step. A little dazed, it took a moment to collect its wits, then hopped quickly down the stairs and off into the grass.

"You're welcome!" I called after it, and then followed Babette inside. Today she offered peach tea and lovely little cookies with walnuts, flavored with cardamom and butter and rolled in powdered sugar.

"I make these," I told her, my voice muffled with sugar.

"Do you, dear? A princess who can cook? That's not usual." She bustled around the kitchen as we spoke, arranging things, tidying up. I had begun to notice that she was rarely still. Even when she sat, her fingers were always moving items on the table, playing with her hair, stroking a cat that appeared from another room and wound itself around our ankles. Her constant movements made me more aware of myself when I moved, and I resolved to sit very still when I sat, just to see if I could.

"I'm not a usual princess," I pointed out. "I live with the maids, downstairs. My father doesn't speak to me."

"Living with the maids can be very useful for a princess, I would think," Babette said.

"Why is that?"

"Well, don't you agree that a ruler should understand her people? And how better to understand them than to live among them?"

I hadn't thought about that. "That's true," I acknowledged. "But I'm never going to be a ruler. I have twelve sisters ahead of me in the succession."

"You may marry a ruler," Babette reminded me. "And even if you don't, your knowledge can help your sister when she rules."

"I could tell her all about the servants!" I said eagerly. "I already do tell them a lot, but not the important things. How the servants feel about working. How they feel about the king. What they want to do or to be. Would those things be useful to Aurelia?"

Babette nodded. "They would indeed," she said. "A ruler who knows what her subjects want—and cares about it—would be a good ruler, in my opinion. Or a better one, at any rate." Then she changed the subject. "And where, my dear, is your friend Breckin?"

"He's supposed to meet me here," I said. "Perhaps he couldn't get away." I was sorry to miss Breckin, but it was nice to have Babette to myself. There were questions I wanted answered that I wasn't sure I wanted to ask in front of Breckin.

I took another cookie and chewed thoughtfully. Then I said, "When we were here before, you said we should come to you 'if anything strange or frightening should happen.' What did you mean by that? What do you think will happen?"

Babette sipped her tea, then picked up her needlework and began to embroider a pillow cover. "Oh, I don't really know, child," she said. "When I saw you coming that day, I just had a feeling. . . . Most likely, I was all wrong. It's been a long time since I looked into a divining bowl, and I had a terrible time reading it ."

"A divining bowl?" It sounded fascinating, and a little frightening.

"It's just water in a bowl, no more. The words you say over it are what gives it power."

"Oh, please, show me!" I pleaded. It sounded very exciting.

Babette frowned, an expression that looked very uncomfortable on her face. It pulled her wrinkles in the wrong directions, used as they were to smiling. "I don't know, Zita," she said slowly. "I don't think . . ."

"Please!" I begged. I knew well how to wheedle, having practiced for years on Cook. And Cook was a far harder nut to crack than Babette, who seemed inclined to please me.

"I suppose it can't hurt," she acceded. "Just for a minute, though!"

"Yes, just for a minute!" I agreed, delighted. I scrambled around, collecting the items she bade me: a copper bowl, a pitcher of well water, a midnight blue cloth embroidered with silver stars, a tiny silver pot of what looked like dust, tucked away deep in a cupboard. Babette laid the cloth on the table, placed the bowl atop it, and poured water in to fill it halfway. She spoke words I could not quite hear, moving her hands gracefully over the bowl. As she finished, she picked up a pinch of the dust and scattered it over the water. Then she bowed her head, looking into the bowl, and I looked with her, my heart beating wildly.

We saw nothing at first, and I was preparing to voice my disappointment. Then, suddenly, the surface of the water shuddered. Slowly, as I watched in amazement, I saw a tiny facsimile of the palace build itself over the water, as if the bowl held our lake. It rose up, three-dimensional, with all the familiar curlicues and crenellations, until it towered high above the bowl. The vision shimmered in the air for a moment, and then collapsed back into the water soundlessly.

"Oh!" I gasped. Babette chuckled.

"That, my dear, was only illusion," she said. "That was for fun. Now we'll look inside your home. What would you like to see?"

"Let me see my sisters' room," I suggested. Again we bent over the water and Babette spoke; again she sprinkled the dust across the water. A shape began to shine in the water, and then it faded. Babette spoke once more, sprinkled more dust. Again a shape formed—was it a room? Did I see windows? Before I could tell for sure, it was gone.

"How very strange," Babette murmured. "I'm usually quite good at this. Of course, I've done it very seldom in these two score years, but still . . . one doesn't forget." She tried over and over, with the same result.

"There must be a guard against it," she said, sounding bewildered.

"A guard?" I asked. "You mean someone to prevent you?"

"Not someone—something. A magic that is keeping me from looking."

I was shocked. "There's no magic in the palace! It's the law—there can't be."

"And yet," Babette mused, "there is."

Speechless, I stared at her. The idea that there could be magic all around me, and I had never noticed—it just didn't seem possible. Whose magic? What was it there for? Was it good magic or bad?

"I don't know, child," Babette said, answering my unspoken thoughts in her uncanny way. "I will have to look into it."

"Will you go there?" I asked. I didn't think she should; what if my father saw her? Surely he would know at a glance that she was a witch.

"No, that wouldn't be wise," she agreed. "I will do what I can from here. But you must let me know . . . ."

"If anything strange should happen," I finished for her. "I know. I will. Am I in danger there?"

She pursed her lips. "I shouldn't think so," she said. "It doesn't appear to be something new; it has the feel of old magic to it. If you haven't been harmed before this, I can't see why you would now."

I shook my head in disbelief. Perhaps Babette was

making the whole thing up—it sounded so unlikely. Then I had a thought. "If it's old, maybe it was just left behind from before Father made the law," I suggested.

"Perhaps," Babette replied in a tone that sounded to me as if she had barely heard me.

"Well, can you show me something else? Can you show me where Breckin is?" I asked. "Maybe we can find out why he didn't come."

"Yes. Let's try again," Babette agreed. I was feeling very doubtful by now, and I wanted a chance to see whether she could actually do magic at all. There was the frog, of course, but perhaps that was the simplest kind of spell, one nearly anyone could do. This would be harder, I was sure.

Babette did her motions and spoke her words, and the water shimmered as we peered into it. Then a picture began to form. It was not the stables, as I had expected, but a clearing in the woods. I could see the trees as plain as day, each bare branch and fallen acorn. There, sitting on a log and shivering, was Breckin. He was obviously lost.

"Oh dear," Babette said, and I giggled.

"I guess he couldn't picture the path," I said smugly. Babette frowned at me, and I quickly said, "Should we go look for him?"

"*You* should," Babette said pointedly. "It is getting

late." I nodded, feeling a little ashamed. I pulled on my shawl and stood to go.

"C-can I—," I stammered. "May we come back?" I looked at the floor. I felt the weight of Babette's disapproval, and I wasn't sure I understood. What had I done wrong?

"You must always think of how others feel," Babette told me. "Try to put yourself in Breckin's place. How would you feel?"

I was embarrassed—and slightly offended. "I thought of the frog," I reminded her. "I knew it did not want to be a door knocker."

"You must think not only of frogs but of other people," Babette said firmly. So I thought about Breckin, sitting alone in the forest. Perhaps he had been walking for hours. If it were me, I would be tired, hungry, thirsty. Afraid.

"I'll find him," I promised. "I'm sorry."

Babette smiled. "Come visit again," she said. "The days are short, and the cold makes me lonely."

I kissed her, relieved, and hurried out of the cottage. When I got to the edge of the clearing where it sat, I looked back to see its ruined self and marveled at the illusion. Then I walked on, trying to envision the place where I had seen Breckin in the divining bowl. I had hoped that by picturing that place, I would be led to it, as had happened with Babette's cottage. But it didn't work, so I called Breckin's name as loudly as I could and was soon rewarded with an answering cry. I stumbled through the underbrush and found him sitting on the log I had seen in the bowl, shivering and irritated.

"Where have you been?" he demanded.

"I? I was at Babette's house. Where were you?"

He scowled. "I kept trying to picture the path, and I couldn't seem to hold it in my mind. I'd think I had it, and then I would walk into a tree. I fell into a stream. I got caught in brambles." He looked at me. "You mean to say that you could do it?"

I shrugged, pleased. "It was easy." Then I remembered what Babette had said to me about thinking of how others feel. "Well, not easy, exactly. But I think it gets easier when you practice. And next time, we'll go together. That way, whichever of us can do it can lead the way."

Breckin sighed and stood. "Well, at least I can get us out of the woods. You'd be lost in here trying to get back."

I nodded, smiling to myself. Boys were so proud—you always had to let them think they were good at things. I'd noticed this with the various fire boys I'd played with over the years. They needed to think that they were the best at spinning tops or running races. If I won a contest, they would sulk, sometimes for days. And I rarely would let them win, so we were often at odds with each other. But Breckin was right, after all—I always did get lost in the forest. And I was glad to have him to help me find my way back. So glad, in fact, that when I reached out to pull him up from the log where he sat, I kept my hand in his. We stood for a moment, palm to palm. I blushed, and I could see my blush reflected in Breckin's red cheeks. We did not let go, but swung our hands between us as we started back.

As we walked, I told him about what had happened at the cottage. He was impressed by my description of the divining bowl, and his eyes grew wide when I told him about what had happened when Babette tried to look into the palace.

"There's magic there?" he said. "Why? Whose magic?"

"We couldn't tell," I told him. "You seem to have the ability to sense magic. Why didn't you know about it?"

"Well," he said hesitantly, "I've . . . I've never actually been in the palace, except for the time you doctored my scrape." He looked a little embarrassed.

"Really!" I exclaimed. "Never? Not even for a meal?" Most of the servants took their meals together in the kitchen, though I ate as Cook and I worked, so I rarely joined them. But now that I thought on it, I didn't recall ever seeing Breckin at the long, scarred wooden table where everyone sat down to their evening food—or anywhere else inside the palace.

"I eat in the stables," he said. "The horses seem to like it when I do—unless it's venison. They get nervous when I eat that."

I was wondering why that would be when we emerged from the trees. The setting sun tinged the stone of the palace with pink and lavender, and it looked like one of Cook's fanciest cakes, beribboned with icing.

"We'd better separate," I said, and at last he let go of my hand. It had become a little damp and numb, but I did not mind. I cradled it as if it were a thing separate and special as we set off in different directions, me to the palace, Breckin back to the stables. As soon as he was out of sight, I realized that we had not set a time and place to meet again, and I thought about following him to do so. But I feared being seen—that would surely mean an end to any friendship I might have with him. So I decided to bide my time, sure that we could cross paths soon.

That Sunday, my sisters seemed tired and listless. I thought perhaps it was because the cold weather was setting in and they were trapped inside more and more. They still rode when the sun shone, but the cold prevented them from boating, picking apples and berries, and engaging in the other outdoor activities that they enjoyed in the warmer months. Akila complained of a headache, and Asenka said that her legs hurt her. None of them seemed inclined to do my hair or try out their pink powder on my cheeks, nor did they want me to put on dresses from their great closet.

"I just want to sleep," Amina moaned, and the others nodded. Were they getting sick? I was worried and laid my hand on Amina's head as I had seen Nurse do when Aurelia had scarlet fever and Allegra had measles. But her forehead was cool and dry, though her eyes were a little swollen.

"You've been reading too much," I scolded her. "I'll read to you tonight for a change." I took up the nearest book and began reading the story of the Goose Girl, who held conversations with the head of her dead horse. It was a gruesome tale, but its nastiness wasn't enough to keep my sisters awake. Before long, their gentle snores made me look up from a gilt-edged illustration of the horse's head, mounted on a wall, and I saw that all twelve of them were sound asleep. Disappointed, I put the book away and waited for Nurse to come in with our nightly snack of hot chocolate.

"Why, they're all tired out!" Nurse said in surprise when she entered. "I hope the poor darlings aren't spoiling for a cold." She clucked around, tucking in covers and smoothing blond locks as I sipped my chocolate.

"I don't think so," I said. "They aren't sniffling, and none of them seems to have a fever."

"That's good," Nurse said. "Perhaps it's just the tiredness of a long, dull day then, poor dearies. Hours at church in the morning, supper with your father, no visitors whatever. Bored to sleep, I'll wager." She shook her head mournfully.

I yawned, feeling their tiredness suddenly myself. "Me too," I said to Nurse, and she chuckled.

"Scoot into bed then, my pet," she told me, and I crawled in beside Akila. Nurse blew out the lamps and shut the door as she went out, and I knew no more.

The next day I was full of energy from my early night. I had left my sisters at dawn and snuck downstairs as I usually did, and I did not see them until midafternoon, when they were at a deportment lesson in the dining room and I was told by Cook to bring tea to Master Beolagh.

"He'll not be with us much longer," Chiara, who had come down for her own tea, pointed out. "He couldn't make the princesses speak, that one. He's no good at all!" Her eyes gleamed with pleasure at the thought of his dismissal.

When I entered the room with the tea tray, my sisters, oddly, showed no sign that they knew me or had any interest in the tea. They were seated around the long table, slumped in tired and very unladylike positions, and Master Beolagh, too silly to know that his job was in peril, was visibly annoyed with them.

"Tea, ladies," he said pointedly, which was a signal for Aurelia to pour, as she was the eldest. Aurelia stared down at her hands clasped in her lap and gave no sign of having heard.

"Princess Aurelia!" Master Beolagh shouted, clapping his hands. The sudden noise in the silent room startled everyone, and the cups rattled as I trembled. I set the tray on the table and backed quietly away, but I was not yet at the door when Master Beolagh said, "I don't know what is wrong with you ladies today. Your comportment is dull and lifeless, and your manners are lacking entirely! Don't you recall the lesson on boredom from my book *Deportment for Princesses*? I quote: 'If you are bored at a social occasion'—and surely you ladies must be bored, or else why would you be so entirely lackluster?—'you must disguise your dullness and appear as interested as if you were experiencing the most fascinating of people at the most fascinating of events.' I do not see that happening here, ladies. Your dullness is not in the least disguised!"

I could barely keep from laughing, and I looked to catch Adena's eye and share a smile with her. But Adena, too, stared at her lap, and her face was drawn and tired. The concern that I had felt the day before came back stronger than ever. I hurried out the door and went looking for Nurse.

I found her in the princesses' bedroom, straightening up their combs and brushes. "Nurse," I said without preamble, "are my sisters ill?"

She spun around, startled at my presence. "Zita!" she said. "What do you ask, dearie?"

"Are they sick? They seem pale and tired—they aren't themselves at all."

Nurse shook her head. "I don't think so, my pet. I haven't noticed anything amiss. I'll look to it, though. They were tired yesterday. Perhaps a dose of the castor oil . . ."

I backtracked hurriedly. "Oh, I don't think they need that. I'm sure it's nothing. Just a touch of . . ." What? Sun—this late in the year? Hay fever—after the first frost? I could think of nothing. I just knew that if they were aware I'd been the cause of a dose of castor oil, they'd never forgive me.

"Don't worry, dearie," Nurse said, smiling. "I won't say a word about you. And don't you worry about them, either. I'm sure they're fine."

I did not see the princesses again until the following Sunday night. They did not go out at all, but spent
the days in their room, resting. I spent a frustrating
week trying to see both them and Breckin, but there
was always something preventing me. Cook had endless chores, for though we did not entertain, Father still
required feasts' worth of food for the various autumn
celebrations. The cold settled in seriously, and I was
glad to be confined to the kitchen most days, for the
great fires kept the room dry and warm when the rest
of the palace ranged from damp and chill to damp and
freezing.

On Sunday night I sat in the dumbwaiter and waited
to be pulled upward, but nothing happened. I yanked
on the cord, my usual signal, but there was no answering
yank. I tried to pull myself upward, and at first strained
mightily, achieving nothing. Finally, with a groan, the
dumbwaiter began to rise very slowly. I paused after
every few moments, frightened that if I let my grasp of
the rope loosen the dumbwaiter would plunge downward. Up and up I pulled, my muscles aching and
throbbing. If I hadn't been strong from carrying wood,
kneading dough, and rolling out crusts, I never could
have done it, but after what seemed an hour, I arrived
in my sisters' closet.

I tumbled out of the dumbwaiter and stepped into

the bedroom. All was silent. The candles burned low, and my sisters slept, one to a bed, in the still room. I could barely hear their breathing; even Asenka, who often snored, was quiet.

I went to Asmita's bed. I was to stay with her tonight. "Asmita!" I whispered, near to her ear. She didn't move. I was suddenly struck with a nameless terror, and I stepped back and stared hard at the coverlet over her. As I watched, it rose, then fell with her breath, and I breathed deeply in relief myself.

I wandered the room aimlessly. Because I had waited so long to be pulled up, Nurse had already come with our chocolate. I poured myself a cup, wincing as the heat of the cup touched my hands, raw from the dumb-waiter rope. As I sipped, I walked over to the window and stood looking out. A cold moon, masked with cloud, shone above in the sky and below in the lake water, and I thought how on my embroidered coverlet, I stood at the exact same spot in the same window. Then I remembered the shadow that seemed to stand behind me on the embroidered cloth, and a shiver ran up my spine. I stood very still, suddenly convinced that some-one stood behind me. The room was noiseless, but I felt sure that I could hear breathing just by my shoulder. I spun around fast, spraying chocolate in an arc, and saw—nothing. Just the rows of beds, the dressing gowns tossed over chairs or bed frames, the slippers placed by Nurse hopefully beside each bed. But was that a sound outside, in the hall?

I tiptoed to the door and opened it carefully, quietly. It squeaked on its hinges, and I cringed. When I had it open far enough that I could peer out, I saw Chiara disappearing down the stairs, and I wondered what she was doing up and about so late. The corridor was empty but for the line of my sisters' shoes, placed outside for cleaning and repair. Embroidered cloth, butter-soft leather, gleaming buckles, bows, silk flowers, French heels—the shoes stood side by side like small sentinels, guarding my sisters' door.

"Was it just Chiara?" I whispered to them, feeling a little foolish.

I closed the door softly and padded between the beds to Asmita's. As I climbed in, rubbing my cold feet against her sleep-warmed ones, I felt an overwhelming drowsiness come over me. The next thing I knew it was dawn, and I had to leave.

Chapter 6
In Which I Take Action

s the next week passed, my sisters seemed to grow still paler and weaker. They did not even come downstairs for their lessons, for when they tried to climb the stairs, they were so slow and feeble that Nurse declared they must not leave their chamber except for Sunday services. Master Beolagh, no longer needed, was sent packing, much to Chiara's glee, and the other tutors took their leave as well. Cook made up little treats for the princesses, and Nurse had us boil up some tinctures of herbs and smelly teas. Meals came back untouched, and the atmosphere in the palace began to be one of anxious waiting.

Then on Sunday morning, at chapel, Adena, always the most delicate of my sisters, fainted. She stood for the Kiss of Peace, and suddenly, gracefully, she collapsed. Alanna screamed, and all of us below their balcony looked up to see Adena draped over the railing. Quickly the service halted, servants were dispatched, and Adena was carried out.

I was frantic. Cook said I could not go up to the bedroom, but I chafed under her stern eye until she relented at last, sending me up with a pot of chocolate "in case the poor things will take any nourishment at all." I ran, as fast as I could without spilling, up the marble staircases and down the long hall to my sisters' room. The door stood open and the room was full of activity, but I did not notice in all the ruckus, until it was too late, that at the center of it all was my father.

In my shock I let the tray in my hands become unbalanced, and the pot of chocolate began to slide. I righted it with a gasp and a rattle of cups, and everyone in the room turned from Adena's bed to stare at me. I felt my father's eyes on me, and again the tray wobbled. Aurelia came to my rescue; she plucked the tray from my hands and set it on a little inlaid marble table, saying, "Oh, thank you, Zita. This is just what we need. Father, will you take some chocolate?"

Father shook his head with disdain. "This is a

sickroom," he said firmly. "No one should be here but the princesses, the doctor, and me."

My sisters moved toward me, surrounding me. I could see us reflected in the great mirror on the wall, and saw what my father must have seen: my own rude, ruddy form beside my sisters' limp paleness. My good health and high color made them look all the more wan and wasted. But ill as they were, my sisters stood beside me as if daring my father to expel me from the room. My heart warmed as I felt them pressing against me.

"Zita has just brought us chocolate, Father," Aurelia said smoothly. "We will not disturb Dr. Valentin. We will just sit over here and drink our chocolate and wait."

"Then do so, and be quiet," Father said crossly. "You twitter like a flock of birds. This child needs rest and quiet!" He stood aside as Dr. Valentin worked over Adena. I felt all the more anxious for the doctor's presence; he only came to the palace in times of great emergency, as when Amina broke her arm when she fell trying to balance on a crossbeam in the stable, or when Allegra, long ago, had developed pneumonia and we had thought she would die. As we waited, my sisters barely touched their chocolate, each picking up her cup and bringing it to her lips, then lowering it untasted.

Finally the doctor stood back, wiping his hands on a

cloth. Under the bedclothes, Adena's small body barely made a bump.

"She has an excess of melancholy," Dr. Valentin announced. "I shall have to bleed her to restore a balance."

I felt panicked. Even I could see that the last thing Adena needed was to be bled. She was so pale and weak now that to lose blood might kill her. Luckily, Father thought the same.

"Nonsense, man!" he said. "You know I don't hold with bleeding. The girl's not melancholic, she's ill. It's your job to find out what's wrong with her!"

The doctor looked very nervous. His mop of gray hair flopped back and forth as he shook his head at my father's stubbornness.

"Your Majesty, I have looked for all the signs of illness. She has no fever, no swellings, no untoward cuts or scrapes, no infection of any sort. Her hair is not falling out, nor are her eyes yellowed. Her throat is pink, not red, and she exhibits no signs of pain, except for the blisters on her feet, and they are not infected. I have concluded melancholy and prescribed bloodletting because I can find evidence of no other problem."

My father hated that. He liked an answer to a problem, and a solution that would work, and he liked it *now*. The veins on his neck stood out. Dr. Valentin nervously picked up his bag and hurried toward the door, bowing to us as he passed. "Princesses," he murmured, "eat more red meat." And he was gone. He'd not be paid for this visit, poor man.

We turned back toward Father, expecting an outburst, but he was looking down at Adena, small and silent on the bed. Aurelia hurried to them and put her hand on Father's shoulder. He turned to her, and I could see worry on his face—a look I certainly had never seen there before. I was envious. Why could I not be sick and in my bed, for Father to look like that over me? But then I felt guilty for my envy, and my sensibility won out. I knew that even if I were sick to death, Father would not look like that. Not for me. Still, I was glad that he could worry for Adena. It hinted that there was still human feeling in him.

"Daughters," Father said, "you must all take care of yourselves. You must rest, and not study so hard. You do not look well." My sisters cast their eyes downward, embarrassed. He went on. "I do not wish to see you ill, like your sister, do you understand?" My sisters nodded as one. "And as the doctor has nothing useful to recommend, I will ask you and your nurse to take care of Adena. Give her possets and porridge, and keep her away from drafts. Can you be counted on to do that?" Again they nodded.

I was growing angry. Adena did not have an ague; she did not need to be kept away from drafts and fed porridge. There was something truly wrong with her. Perhaps she was dying! Why were my sisters so timid? But then my father's glance fell again on me, and I remembered why. His attention was imposing, his gaze piercing.

"Zita, you bring sickness from the lower reaches," he scolded me. "Stay out of the chambers until this malady has passed. Confine your work to the kitchen." I too stared at the floor, but I could feel my face redden and see my fists clench. I could not stay belowstairs when my sisters were sick! Still, like my sisters and like the servant I was, I nodded and curtsied and stumbled to the door and out into the hallway.

Outside the bedchamber, I took a deep breath—my first deep breath, I realized, since I had entered that room. I shook my head to rid it of the stuffiness of the chamber. Then I noticed my sisters' shoes in front of me, each pair standing primly matched together. I looked at them and frowned. They seemed in terrible shabby shape. The curved heels were worn unevenly, and the rich fabric and leather uppers were scuffed and threadbare. I picked up a shoe that I recognized as Ariadne's, dark green silk embroidered with roses, and turned it over. The sole was worn to holes. I could see my own hand right through it. I thought back to the previous week, when I had peeked through the door and seen the shoes. Had they been so worn? I didn't remember thinking so. Why were they tattered now? What had happened in that week to wear down the heels and put holes in the soles? It was surpassing strange.

I ran down the stairs and emerged into the kitchen, where the maids were gathered before the warm fire, talking in hushed voices of Adena's collapse.

"What news?" Cook demanded of me. "Did she take the chocolate? You were gone a marvelous long time, Zita!"

I shook my head. "She wasn't awake, I don't think. The doctor was there, but he didn't know what was wrong. He wanted to bleed her—"

"That'll do her good," Cook said, pleased.

"—but the king said no. She's to rest and eat porridge."

"Porridge!" Cook protested. "I've been making her porridge all week, and she hasn't touched a bite." She fulminated, her broad red brow furrowed with the effort of her thought. "Perhaps a dainty, just for her. A little pastry, in the shape of something. What does she like especially, Zita?"

I thought quickly. I wanted to see Breckin badly, to tell him about the shoes and ask his opinion. "She likes walnuts," I said. "I could go and find some. There are still nuts fallen on the forest edge."

"Run then," Cook said agreeably. "We'll make a tiny walnut tart, shaped like a daisy. All the princesses like daisies."

I pulled my cloak from a peg on the wall and dashed out, picking up a small basket on the way. Over the bridge I ran, and then when the path turned toward the stables in one direction and toward the forest in the other, I looked back to see if any eyes were watching me from the palace. I could see no one, so I turned toward the stables.

I found Breckin grooming Father's stallion, Ashwin, currying his deep brown flanks. And when the stallion moved, I stopped in surprise, for on his other side was a man, dressed in the uniform of a soldier. He was tall, with dark auburn hair and a trim beard, and he leaned against the wall comfortably, laughing at something Breckin had said. I saw the stripes on his sleeve and realized with a shock that he was the same captain I'd seen on horseback not long before, the one who had bowed to Aurelia.

I turned to run, fearful that the captain had perhaps been hired as a new guard of Father's and would tell that he'd seen me, but it was too late.

"Zita!" Breckin said, a huge smile on his face. "Look

who is here! This is my brother, Milek, visiting on leave from the Reaches."

Milek bowed, and I dipped automatically into a curtsy, grateful to my sisters for my training in manners.

"Princess," Milek said. "I am honored."

I laughed. "Honored—to meet *me*? Don't be ridiculous."

Milek raised an eyebrow at his brother. "I see you did not exaggerate," he said to Breckin mildly.

I was flustered. "I just meant—I'm sorry. I'm not really a princess. Well, I am. But still—"

"Oh, do be quiet, Zita," Breckin broke in. "He was just being polite."

"Far more so than you!" I snapped, deeply embarrassed. I turned my back on Breckin and faced his brother. "I am pleased to make your acquaintance, sir," I said in my most refined tone. "And how long will you grace us with your presence?"

Milek smiled at me, and I noted that, although he was older than I'd thought at first, with sun-burnished skin and craggy planes and angles to his face, his brown eyes were warm and very handsome—very like Breckin's.

"I am able to stop for only a night or two," he said. "I am on my way home to help our mother for a few days. She is unwell, and I must ready the house for winter.

Then it's back to my duties." He touched a hand to the sword at his side, and I wondered whether he had ever had cause to use it.

"I hope her illness is not serious," I said, looking to see whether Breckin seemed worried.

"I think it is not," Milek replied, "but she cannot manage alone just now, and my sister and her husband are away. So I am needed."

"I've seen you before," I said then. "Two months or so ago, on horseback."

I could see immediately that he remembered, for the color rose in his face.

"Yes, I recall," he said. "It was just after Breckin had begun his employ here. We were patrolling nearby, and I was hoping to see my brother. But instead . . ."

"Instead you saw my sister," I said slyly. Milek did not reply, but only smiled, so I did not speak on it further. After all, he was not Breckin, a mere boy to be teased.

"Perhaps if you come to the kitchen tonight, late, I can find you a morsel or two to eat, and some to take on your journey," I said. "You'll have to be wary crossing the bridge, though. The guard will challenge you if he sees you."

"We men in uniform make allowances for one another," Milek told me. "I'd be glad of some food to take with me. Walking makes me powerfully hungry.

Will . . . will anyone else be there?"

I was puzzled for a moment, but then I remembered the moment of silent communication between him and Aurelia, and I realized that he was thinking of her.

"There will be no one else in the kitchen at that hour," I told him, smiling inwardly.

In the excitement of meeting Milek, I had quite forgotten why I had come to the stables, but Breckin asked me, "What brings you down here, Zita?"

"Oh!" I said, my hands flying to my cheeks. "I'd wanted to ask—maybe you can tell me. There's something very odd happening with my sisters. Does this sound like magic to you?" I told them about Adena, and my sisters' exhaustion, and the shoes, and they looked concerned.

"Are all the princesses affected?" Milek asked. Again, I looked at him, knowing to whom he referred.

"All are tired and seem ill," I said, "but only Adena is bedridden."

"It does sound like magic, if the doctor can find no illness," Milek said.

Breckin nodded. "And not a good kind, either. If Babette saw magic in the palace, perhaps it's directed against your sisters. Or against Adena, in particular. Do you know anyone who doesn't like her?"

I shrugged helplessly. "Who would she know? She

sees no one—none of them do. Only peddlers and beggars and men on the king's business come to the palace."

Milek put a comforting hand on my shoulder. "When I come tonight, perhaps I can better judge. Will you bring me to the princesses?"

I gulped. It would be dangerous, and terribly improper. But I would do anything for my sisters, and somehow I felt that Milek could be trusted. I nodded.

"I'll be there at moonrise," he promised.

Grateful, I clasped his hand, and then I sped back to the palace, stopping only to get a few nuts for Adena's tart.

The moon rose late that night, and I could see the trail it made on the still waters of the lake as I watched through the kitchen window for Milek. I saw his tall, lean figure stride across the land bridge, and I panicked for a moment when the guard stepped forward to challenge him. They spoke briefly, and then the guard clapped Milek on the back and allowed him into the palace.

I met him at the kitchen door. "What did you tell the guard?" I asked, curious.

Milek looked a little abashed. "Well . . . I said that I was meeting a serving girl. I meant no disrespect—it was just a story to get me past."

I laughed. "I am not offended," I said. "It was clever, and it did the job. And here you are, and here are some roast lamb and new potatoes left over from dinner!"

Milek sat at the long kitchen table, and I sat opposite him and watched as he ate like a man half starved. He slowed when he came to the slice of tart I cut him.

"Ah," he sighed. "The lamb is like my mother's cooking, but this tart! I have never tasted its like."

I was very pleased. "I made that," I said, attempting a modest look.

"A princess who can bake!" he exclaimed, echoing Babette's earlier words. "You are unique, milady."

I blushed and smiled, and with that, Milek and I were friends.

When Milek had finished eating, I gave him a packet of bread and cheese and the rest of the tart, wrapped carefully for traveling. He stowed it in his pack, slung it over his shoulder, and then stood.

"Now show me your sisters," he said.

He followed me as I tiptoed to the pantry. When I removed the sacks hiding the dumbwaiter and signaled him that we would both get in, his eyebrows went up just as Breckin's often did. He followed me without a word. We pulled ourselves up as silently as possible, and when we reached the princesses' closet, we crept out.

I eased the closet door open. The room was dim and

silent, but a swathe of moonlight made its way through the heavy curtains and fell across the floor. We could make out the twelve beds, each with its sleeping girl. The faint sound of breathing was the only noise.

Gingerly we walked between the rows of beds, and when he reached Adena's, I stopped and pointed. We watched her for a time, and I noted how slow her breaths were. At last Milek nodded, and we turned to go. But one of the girls had left a petticoat crumpled beside her bed that Nurse had not picked up, and Milek caught his boot in it and tripped. He caught himself before he fell, but his sword rattled against a bed frame, making a racket that, in that silent room, seemed as loud as a whole army in battle. We froze. In terror I thought of what would happen if we were discovered. The guards would rush in; Milek would face Father's wrath and surely die for his trespass. And I—I would be exiled, at the very least.

But no sister awakened. Not one even stirred. In and out went their breaths in the silence, and their bedclothes rose and fell steadily. Relieved, we quickly started back to the closet. As Milek passed Aurelia's bed, though, he stopped again, very suddenly. I, behind him, almost ran right into him. He stood as if in a trance, looking down at Aurelia's lovely face, illuminated in the moonlight. All breath in the room seemed to pause.

As I watched, I saw to my shock that Aurelia's eyes were open. She gazed straight back at Milek with what seemed like recognition, and her lips parted as if she were going to speak, but no words came out. A look passed between them that echoed the one I had seen months before, and a moment later Aurelia's lashes swept down and she slept again. But a smile played upon her lips, and I saw a matching smile steal quickly across Milek's face.

In the dumbwaiter on the way down, Milek was pale as he worked the ropes to lower us. He was quiet as we placed the potato sacks to hide the door. Back in the vast kitchen, I confronted him.

"Well?" I demanded. "Is it magic? Can you tell?"

Milek nodded, his brow furrowed. "I am no wizard," he said, "but the smell and feel of magic are thick in that room. Your sisters did not wake when I stumbled. That noise would have waked the—would have waked anyone."

Would have waked the dead was what he did not say. I shivered and fought back tears.

"What will happen to them?" I cried "Who is doing this? Oh, Milek, what shall I do?"

"Shh, shh," he cautioned me. "You have a witch friend; you must go to her. Surely she will know what to do. You must consult her."

"Can't you help?" I begged.

He was torn, I could see it. But he shook his head. "I must get home. There is work to do there, and my mother has great need of me. But I will come back, as soon as I can. If the circumstances were any other . . ."

I nodded. He had made a promise, and to his mother. He was a man of honor. I remembered Salina once saying, "A man who treats his mother well is a good man indeed—and a rare one!"

"Then Breckin and I will go to Babette," I said. "Will you tell him to meet me at the stream, where we picnicked?" Milek nodded, and I led him to the corridor. At the doorway, I gave him my hand, and he bent over it like a courtier. When he straightened, I could see a question in his eyes, and I forestalled him.

"Her name is Aurelia," I said. "She is my eldest sister. She is not betrothed."

He grinned—Breckin's grin again—bowed smartly, and was gone.

I spent all the next morning trying to find a chance to run upstairs and see my sisters. The chance did not come; Cook had heard of my father's rule forbidding me access to their chamber, and she did her best to keep me busy so I couldn't sneak off. When her back was turned as she rolled out dough, however, I grabbed a hot meat pie, a towel to wrap it in, and my cloak and ran out and across the bridge, not looking back to see who might be watching me. I didn't take a deep breath until the woods had swallowed me from view, and then I slowed to a quick walk, noting familiar landmarks as I moved along. Without much trouble I found my way back to the pretty spot where Breckin and I had picnicked. Now the stream was rimmed with ice, though its swift waters still flowed unfrozen. The willow's branches were bare and brown, and I clapped my hands together and moved from foot to foot as I waited, trying to keep warm. It wasn't long before Breckin appeared. We shared the meat pie, still warm from Cook's oven, and we talked about what had happened when Milek and I had visited my sisters' bedchamber.

"He was strange when he came back," Breckin said.

I smiled. "He was not strange. He was in love."

Breckin choked on a piece of meat pie. "In love?" he said, coughing. "With who? You?"

I felt a stab of hurt at his incredulity. Was it so unbelievable that someone should love me? I turned on Breckin, hot anger rising to overcome the hurt, but before I could get a word out, he caught my hands in his.

"I'm sorry," he said swiftly. "I did not mean that the way it sounded. Forgive me?" He looked pleadingly, contritely, into my eyes, and I found myself gazing back. The look he gave me was unfamiliar. I was suddenly unable to speak. He moved toward me, and I thought in a panicked rush, *I am going to be kissed!* And then I remembered my promise to Aurelia. I could not. I would not.

I pulled back, flushed and flustered, and mumbled, "It's all right. Of course it is not me. It's Aurelia. He looked on her, and he loved her. Who would not?"

Breckin gaped, and his shocked face made me laugh. Suddenly we were ourselves again. "Yes, he aims high, doesn't he?" I teased, rising from the fallen log where we sat. "But I promised Aurelia that I would find her a husband, and he is a fine-looking, brave soldier!"

"That's ridiculous," Breckin sputtered. "He's a commoner, the son of a farmer."

I shrugged. "My father would never let her marry him, it's true. But perhaps he can steal her away, under cover of night. They can go back to your mother's farm and tend the bees together. Or Aurelia could travel with Milek's company, cooking for her captain over a campfire."

Breckin burst out laughing at this, and I knew he was picturing my elegant sister, her golden sheaf of hair perfectly groomed, her luxurious clothes always spotless—crouched over a smoky fire, frying up sausages.

As we neared the place where I thought Babette's cottage stood, I placed my hand on Breckin's arm and said, "Stop. Right here. Now close your eyes." He did as I said.

"Good. Now, picture the path. White stones, lined with flowers. No, not flowers now. Pretty purple cabbages. Up to a white cottage with lace at the windows. Can you see it?"

Breckin breathed hard with the effort. "Almost," he said. "Yes. Just how it looked from the inside looking out, but with cabbages."

I nodded. "Keep your eyes closed. Walk forward slowly, so you don't trip." I closed my own eyes and took his hand and we both walked forward. Dead leaves crunched under our feet, and then we heard pebbles move against our boots. I opened my eyes.

"There!" I said, delighted. And there it was, the little cottage, just as I had pictured it, cabbages and all. Breckin whooped and ran up the path, jumping up the stairs. I followed him. The frog knocker was no longer there, so we used our knuckles, and in a moment Babette opened the door, smiling hugely, and invited us in. We crowded into the cozy warmth of the room and held our hands out to the fire burning merrily on the hearth. Babette brought us spiced orange tea and gingerbread, and we sat at the kitchen table and ate and drank until we were full and warm.

Finally we sat back, and Babette said, "So, my dears, what brings you? I feel that this is not merely a friendly visit."

Breckin looked to me to speak. I swallowed the last of my gingerbread and said, "No, it's not merely friendly. There is something wrong, just as you warned. I don't know what it is. I'm hoping you will know."

"Tell me," Babette urged.

I described my sisters' lethargy, their exhaustion and shadowed eyes, their lack of appetite, their worn and tattered shoes. I told her about Adena's faint, the doctor's inability to make a diagnosis. I described my visit to the bedchamber with Milek, the stillness of the sleepers, Aurelia's momentary waking. I even mentioned the princesses' strange encounters with suitors and how they could not speak to the princes who came to call. Babette's brow furrowed, and her nose moved even closer to her chin as she frowned and thought.

"We think it's magic," Breckin said.

"Magic, to be sure. You are right, lad," she said to Breckin. "An enchantment, perhaps. Something strong, and strange." She turned to me. "When you stayed with them, those last two Sundays, did anything unusual happen? Did they sleep through the night? Were they restless?"

"I don't know," I admitted. "I was so tired those nights—I fell right asleep and didn't wake till morning. They were all asleep before I slept, and still sleeping when I woke, though. I don't see how they could have risen without waking me."

"Did you eat or drink before sleep?" she demanded.

I thought. "Well . . . yes. We always have hot chocolate before bed. I had some both nights."

Babette nodded. "Ah," she said, but no more.

Breckin cleared his throat. "Do you think—," he said, and broke off. He started again. "Do you think that . . . that someone put something in the chocolate?"

"What do you mean?" I demanded.

"I mean, a sleeping potion. Something like that?"

I was horrified. Who would do such a thing? Someone in the kitchen, a servant whom I'd worked with? Salina, Dagman, maybe Chiara? The nasty underbutler, Burle? These were people I'd known all my life. It was unthinkable that one of them was working magic, and using it to put people to sleep. To put *me* to sleep!

"Oh, I don't think so," I began. But then I started to wonder. I had been so very tired, but not until I had drunk from my cup. I hadn't woken all night, even though I'd spent one of those nights with Asmita, the twitchiest of my sisters. Usually sleeping with her was like sleeping with one of the hunting pups, which would writhe and moan in its sleep, legs churning as if it were out in the fields running after a rabbit. But I had slept like a stone, deep and dreamless.

"It is possible, my dear," Babette said gently. "We

can assume certain things. One, your sisters are doing something at night. They are not sleeping, so they are exhausted. They are wearing out their shoes, so perhaps they are walking far, in an enchanted place. Two, someone does not want you to find out about it. Your chocolate is drugged to make you sleep."

"But . . . why?" I said, aghast. "Why would anyone want to hurt my sisters? Who could be doing it?"

Babette shook her head. "That's the trick question," she said. "I don't know, and I have no way of seeing. I think that is up to you."

I looked at her, puzzled. "You want me to do magic to find out? But I'm not a witch!"

"No," she corrected me. "I don't want you to do magic. I want you to follow them. To find out where they are going."

I shivered. The idea of getting up out of my warm bed at night and following my bewitched sisters to some enchanted place was not one I embraced. But then I thought of Adena, pale and limp in her bed, and I straightened my spine in the chair. "Yes, all right," I said. "I can see that I have to do that. How do I do it?"

Babette smiled approvingly. "Brave girl," she told me, but I did not feel brave. "You will have to avoid drinking the chocolate, of course."

"I can pour it out the window," I suggested.

"If you can do that without being seen, good. Otherwise, use a sponge to soak it up. Then you can discard the sponge, or just leave it till the morning."

I nodded. "Then what?"

"Then you will have to wait until they rise, and follow them—but without being seen. It will not be easy. You can't let them get too far ahead of you."

"All right. Then what?"

"Well . . ." Babette's voice trailed off. She thought for a minute. "Then you just observe. Remember what you see. Notice everything! And come to me. Tell me what has happened."

"I will," I promised. I closed my eyes, willing panic away. I was not a courageous person. I knew nothing about enchantments or magic. The idea of following my sisters to whatever had been sapping their strength, taking their liveliness and replacing it with fatigue and deathlike sleep, terrified me.

"Can Breckin come?" I said in a low voice, opening my eyes.

"Well, of course I'll come," Breckin said forcefully. "You try to keep me away! It sounds like a good adventure."

Babette smiled, but her smile did not reach her worried eyes. "Oh, it will be an adventure. But a good one? We can only hope so." She stood up and went to the kitchen, rattling around in one of the drawers. When she came back, she carried what looked like a stick. She handed it to me.

"This is a torch, a light-stick," she said. "I know, it doesn't look like one, but you can light it if you have need of light. You have to visualize the light as you did the path—think of the torch lit, picture it lit, and it shall be lit."

I turned the stick around, looking for evidence of its power, but it was nothing more than a piece of wood. I passed it to Breckin.

"It's hickory," he observed. "Doesn't look like much."

"Well, there's truth in the old adage 'Looks can be deceiving,'" Babette told him. "There's truth in most of the old adages."

"Don't you have something more . . . more useful?" I complained. "A cloak of invisibility, perhaps? A spell that will turn us into rocks if need be?"

"You are both quick studies," Babette said. "You can do a certain kind of magic with your own minds, if you practice. It's like finding my house, or lighting the torch—you have to imagine you are something else. Try to feel the essence of what you are becoming. See your-self as that thing. You won't actually become it, but to searching eyes, you might seem close enough that they will pass right over you."

I looked at her in disbelief.

"It's true," she told me. "It's something that some ordinary people have always done. The very best hunters and fishers can do it, and trackers too. They become that which they seek, or they nearly become it. It helps them track and get close, undetected."

"All right," I said doubtfully. "We'll try it. And we'll come back next week and tell you all."

"Good luck, my dears," Babette said. Her tone, anxious and a little uncertain, made my heart sink. What was it we were going to do, if it made a witch sound like that?

Breckin and I trudged back through the woods. The way seemed familiar now. I stole a look at him from time to time and couldn't help wishing that he were more knightly, more grown, better versed with a sword. A boy who was not yet a man wasn't going to be much help if we found ourselves in trouble. But then I saw his set jaw and the determination in his eyes, and I knew that if something bad were to happen, Breckin would defend me as no one else would.

Before we'd reached the edge of the wood, Breckin said, "Maybe we should try it."

"Try what?"

"What Babette said. Try to become something else. Or nearly. I don't know. I don't really understand it."

"*I* don't really believe it," I said. "But I suppose we can try. Here, you go off into that thicket"—I pointed—"and I'll stay here. You try first. I'll give you five minutes."

I danced around to stay warm as I counted off the seconds. Five minutes seemed exceedingly long and chilly. When I reached three hundred, I started toward the thicket where Breckin had gone. I walked all around the area, but I could not find him. Finally I stood still and called his name.

"I'm right here," he said softly, behind me. I spun around.

"We aren't playing hide-and-seek," I complained, and he grinned.

"I wasn't hiding. I was being a tree."

I gaped at him. "Really? It works?"

"You walked right by me, and you seemed to look right at me. Twice!"

I had to try. Breckin stayed where he was and I walked off a little way. I looked at a holly bush beside me and tried to understand its very holliness. Its red berries, its deep green leaves with their sharp points—I looked at and thought about them, hard. And I thought about my own deep colors, and the parts of myself that were pointed or sharp. I was not a holly bush, but I could be very like one. I was not at all surprised when Breckin walked right by me with a suspicious look on his face, turned around, stared past me, and finally called my name. I stopped being holly and stepped out toward him.

"Oh, very good!" he said admiringly. "I'm glad we can both do it. It makes the brain hurt, though, doesn't it?"

It did, rather. You had to think much harder than was customary, and if you let up for even a moment, you'd return to being completely you and be seen. Still, it was nearly as good as a cloak of invisibility—even better, in a way, as we were doing it ourselves, with our own personal store of nonwitch magic.

We had six days to wait until Sunday. Before we parted, Breckin promised to find a way to get inside the palace Sunday evening. He'd make his way to the kitchen and wait for me there, hidden in the pantry where the dumbwaiter opened.

"I'll practice imagining and get better at it," he assured me. "That way, if anyone seems suspicious of me, I'll just become a lamp or a table leg. Don't worry!"

I shook my head. If Cook saw him, or Father, or anyone else who knew that a stableboy did not belong inside the palace, he might be punished, beaten, even forced to leave. And I could not help my sisters without him.

"Be careful," I pleaded. "Don't let Cook see you. I

must find out what is wrong with my sisters, and I need you to help me. Please."

He nodded, his face somber for once. I was heartened to see that he took our task seriously.

We reached the edge of the forest, and while we were still in the shadow of the trees, Breckin took my hands in his, turning me toward him. "You be careful too," he warned me. Before I knew what was happening, he bent toward me and kissed me on the cheek, his soft lips burning where they touched. I gasped, and he dropped my hands as though they, too, burned. I stared at him, shocked. He looked quite as surprised as I felt, and I saw the red move up his neck to his face as I felt myself blushing. Speechless, he turned and ran off toward the stables, and I stood motionless, my hands cold now that they were without the warmth of his.

Chapter 7

In Which I Go on a Journey

ver the next few days, I continually practiced the disappearing skills Babette had
taught us. I became a sack of flour, and
Cook reached right past me for her rolling pin without noticing me there. I became part of
the sideboard and observed my wan sisters and florid-
faced father during an interminable dinner that made
me gladder than ever that I ate in the kitchen. Even the
courses of meat and fowl and elaborate puddings did
not make up for the long silences, in which the clat-
ter of cutlery (silver, not the pewter we servants used)
seemed to echo in the chilly room. I became part of

the hallway and observed my father as he paced up and down the polished floor outside my sisters' bedroom. The worry on his face warmed me, for I was seeing in his concern less and less of the cruel tyrant I had once thought him. Perhaps, I now realized, he loved my sisters. Perhaps he was human after all. The shock of the idea made me lose my concentration and appear clearly again, and he turned and saw me. His face twisted back into its familiar scowl, and I fled for the stairs.

I tried, in those days, to forget about Breckin's kiss. It had just been a peck on the cheek, I told myself. Not a real kiss at all. I had not broken my promise to Aurelia—had I? I had not invited the kiss. But that did not mean that I hadn't enjoyed it. I grew more and more dismayed the more I tried not to think about it, and I finally took my worry to the maids who were, at least a little, my friends. After supper one night, when Cook had taken herself off to bed and Salina and Bethea, whose room I had once shared, remained at the table, I stayed behind as well. Hesitantly I dug at the wooden table with my thumbnail and blushed as I asked, "If . . . if a boy kisses you, is it your fault?"

The girls turned from their chatter to stare at me, and Salina hooted. "Zita has found herself a fellow at last!"

"No, no!" I protested. "It's not me. I can't tell you who it is. She just needs to know. She feels guilty. She promised . . . her mother that she would not kiss a boy. But he kissed her. Did she do wrong?"

They looked skeptical but considered my question seriously.

"Why would she make her mother such a promise?" Bethea asked. "Does her mother not want her to marry?"

"Well, of course she wants her to marry," I said. "It's just . . . her mother doesn't want any trouble. You know. Before she marries."

Salina shook her head. "A smart girl knows to stop at kissing," she told me, laughing as the pink of embarrassment spread up my neck and overran my face. "But if she made the promise, she should keep it. Still, if the boy took the kiss when the girl was unaware or unwilling, it is not her fault. I don't think she broke the promise."

Bethea agreed. "She should be sure not to see that boy again, though," she warned. "Or she should tell him not to try it again."

"Or she should tell her mother not to make her promise such things!" Salina crowed, and we all three laughed.

"I'll tell her," I promised, knowing that they knew there was no such girl and that they would watch me like hawks to discover the identity of the boy who had kissed me. Still, I felt relieved. It was not my fault. Breckin had caught me unawares, and I had not really broken my promise. And it would not happen again.

The week passed with agonizing slowness. I berated myself for waiting so long to put our plan into action, but I could not contact Breckin to change it. Worry about my sisters consumed me. Dawn would find me wide awake, and the crawl of the sun across the sky, short as it was in wintertime, seemed to take forever. Then at night I could not sleep for imagining what would happen on Sunday. By that day I was a nervous, twitchy wreck. I wiggled so much during prayers that Cook kicked me, hard. I put salt rather than sugar in the pie crust, and it baked so hard in the oven that when I took it out it could not be removed from the pan, and the whole mess had to be thrown out, pan and all. I could not eat supper, and Cook grew so worried over my strange behavior that she threatened to sleep with me that night. I was horrified.

"No, no, I'm fine!" I cried, rushing a spoonful of soup to my mouth to prove my appetite. It scalded my tongue and I choked, spitting it out in a great plume.

"There, you see?" Cook said anxiously, looking around the table. "She cannot eat my good soup! She's spoiling for the ague, I'm sure of it. You need a hot plaster, my girl, and a quiet night."

"A quiet night," I agreed. "That's all, Cook. I'm just

a little tired. I'll go to bed early, and by tomorrow I'll be fine. I promise!"

Cook frowned. "You're only tired? Are you certain? For I'd surely not like to share your bed unless it's needful, the way you toss and turn."

"I'll share it, and keep watch over her," volunteered Phineas, one of the footmen. He sniggered, and the maids giggled, but it was entirely the wrong thing to say in front of Cook. She seemed to swell up like a soufflé, and her red face grew nearly purple as her rage rose. Phineas shrank back, already stammering an apology, but it was too late.

"How dare you!" Cook thundered. "She is a princess of this house, never forget that! If her father knew how disrespectfully you had spoken, he would have you drawn and quartered, you insolent pip!"

I was mortified. My lineage was never mentioned in the kitchen, and I did not wish it to be. I needed everyone belowstairs to treat me like any other maid. If they were thinking *princess* every time I passed, my life would become intolerable. I kept my head down and bit the insides of my cheeks, willing myself not to cry.

"Go on with you," Cook said softly to me.

I stood quickly, then nearly ran from the kitchen. By the time I'd reached my room, I was breathing heavily, and resting on my bed did nothing to calm me. I reached under my mattress for the light-stick Babette had given me, and I clutched it to me. It still looked like nothing more than a stick, and when I thought *light* at it, it refused to cooperate, as it had done all week. I stuck it in the pocket of my apron, lay back, and watched the sun's last light move slowly across my narrow window. When at last I could see the evening star, I got up and opened the little wooden box where I hid my few treasured belongings—earrings and ribbons from my sisters, a lock of my mother's golden hair that Akila had given me months before. I pulled out the bundle I had prepared for tonight. In the bundle was a sponge, as Babette had suggested. There was also a short knife I had snuck from the kitchen. Why I had the knife, I did not want to think.

I had to get to my sisters' room much earlier than usual, to be sure they had not fallen into their drugged sleep or gone wherever it was that they went. And I could not use the dumbwaiter, for the kitchen was still busy and I did not know whom I would find in the bedchamber. I climbed the stairs cautiously, my steps slowing as I reached the top floor and the long hallway that would lead me to my sisters' room. A guard sat in a chair partway down the hall, placed there by my father to watch over my sisters. He nodded to me, knowing that I was not a threat, and I proceeded to the great oaken door of the bedchamber. It was just slightly opened, so I peered inside. The room was quiet, but not silent; I heard rustling and low voices. Not the booming roar of my father, nor the doctor's wheedling tenor. I pushed the heavy door open and slowly slipped in. My sisters were readying themselves for bed, brushing hair, slipping on nightgowns, taking off earrings and necklaces. Nurse bustled among them, taking heavy skirts and laying them flat for folding, working out snags from hair. The room was very much quieter than usual, and when Amina noticed me, there was no outcry, no happy greeting as on Sundays past.

"Oh, Zita," she said, looking at me tiredly as she plaited her hair. "Should you be here?"

I was hurt. "Do you not want me here?" I asked her.

"Well . . ." Her voice trailed off.

Nurse looked up from Ariadne's hair, which she was brushing into a golden waterfall over her shoulders. "Your father said not," she said mildly.

"Nurse!" I exclaimed. "You can't forbid me my sisters!"

"No, Nurse," Aurelia echoed. "Leave her be. She will not disturb us."

Nurse's brow creased. "Adena is no better," she admonished. "And Asmita is failing. These girls need no excitement. They need rest and quiet."

Asmita failing! I ran between the rows of beds to Asmita's side. She lay tucked in already, her face as pale as her silvery hair.

"Zita," she greeted me wanly. "We've missed you."

"Oh, Asmita, are you ill?" I wailed.

"Shhhh," she soothed me. "Not ill, just a little tired. Will you stay with me tonight?" She sat up with difficulty and called, "Nurse, can Zita stay with me? I think it would make me feel ever so much better."

Nurse came over to the bed, frowning. "Child, I don't think . . ."

"I'm cold, Nurse," Asmita said. "And Zita will keep me warm. I need her."

Nurse sighed. She could not refuse her charges anything, ever.

"Zita, you will let her sleep?"

"Of course I will!" I exclaimed. "I'll make sure she sleeps through the night."

"Very well," Nurse allowed. "If you rest quiet, Zita, and don't disturb the poor dear with your tossing and turning." She returned to her brushing and folding, and before long, she was gone, leaving only a few candles flickering on the dressers to light the dimness.

Aurelia went to the table, where a pot of chocolate sat. She poured the warm drink into small cups etched with leaves and flowers, and I ran to pass the cups out to my sisters. We sipped in silence, or rather they sipped. When no one was looking, I slipped the sponge from my bundle. I could not possibly pour my chocolate out the window without attracting attention, so I tipped the cup over the sponge and then put the sponge, now dark with chocolate and full, under Ariadne's bed.

Nurse came back to collect our empty cups and placed them on a tray. We climbed into bed, I beside a shivering Asmita, and Aurelia blew out the candles and crawled beneath her own covers. Nurse departed, and within moments, the room was silent but for the gentle breathing of twelve sleeping girls. My breath, though, came fast and ragged as I waited to see what would happen.

Time passed at a crawl. The night was eerily still, for my sisters did not move in their sleep. Their breathing continued quiet, almost inaudible. Nobody turned over; nobody seemed to dream. I heard the little ceramic clock on the mantel chime ten, then eleven. Then midnight.

As the twelfth chime struck, Asmita sat up beside me. My heart leaped in my throat, and I looked through slitted eyes to see the other eleven sitting up as well. Even Adena sat upright, and I saw her and the others push off their bedcovers and stand. Without a word, they moved as one to the closet. There they took out dresses—fancy

embroidered dresses, deep blue and green and plum velvet, silver satin, pink watered silk, which they wore only
for special occasions. They clothed themselves in silence,
helping one another with lacings and hooks and buttons,
then dressed their hair with ropes of pearls and diadems
and silk ribbons. They draped jewels about their necks,
dabbed perfume and adjusted skirts, and finally, they
put on shoes. Even in the dim candlelight, I could see
that these shoes were new: beautifully made, with French
heels and beading, velvet leaves and flowers, dyed in colors to match their gowns. At last they stood, as beautiful
as twelve girls could be, but their eyes were lifeless and
their cheeks white as snow.

I lay like a stone, afraid to breathe too deeply. I knew
for certain now that there was an enchantment, and that
my sisters all were possessed by it. I could only follow and
watch and hope to learn the why and wherefore of it.

I heard a creaking noise, and through my lashes I
saw my sisters going two by two into the closet. They
did not reappear. I realized they must be taking the
dumbwaiter down to the kitchen, and I winced when
I thought of Breckin, hiding amidst the potato sacks. I
hoped he would have the sense to remain hidden when
the dumbwaiter began to discharge the girls.

As the number left in the bedchamber dwindled, two
by two, I began cautiously to rise from the bed. Slowly,

carefully, I pulled on my own clothes and worn boots. My sisters were focused intently on the closet and did not look back at me. As Anisa and Asmita, the last pair remaining, climbed into the dumbwaiter, I reached the closet door and watched them descend out of my sight.

As soon as the dumbwaiter ropes were slack again, I pulled with all my might. I was strong enough now to bring the dumbwaiter up, and I climbed in and lowered myself to the kitchen. There, I tumbled out, whispering, "Breckin! Which way did they go?"

Breckin emerged from among the sacks, shaking his head. "Which way did who go?"

I danced up and down, anxious and not in the mood for teasing. "My sisters, you fool! We must follow them!"

He shook his head again. "They did not come out, Zita," he told me. "I heard the dumbwaiter, but it did not stop here."

I snapped at him, "What do you mean? Where did it stop? Did they get off upstairs?"

He shrugged helplessly. "I don't think so. It sounded like—it sounded like it went down."

"Down!" I whispered. "Down! But that's impossible! Below the kitchen is just . . . water. How could they go down?"

"I don't know," Breckin replied, "but we had better go after them if we want to keep them in sight."

I did not like the sound of this at all. I could swim a little, but I knew that Alanna and Alima could not; in fact, Alima was terribly afraid of the water. And it was wintertime—the lake would be freezing. Still, I knew Breckin was right. Wherever they were going, we had to follow.

We climbed into the dumbwaiter, and I pulled the ropes to lower us. I was expecting nothing whatever to happen—I knew we were on the ground floor. I knew we could not descend. But the dumbwaiter began to move downward. I loosened my grip on the ropes in my shock, and we tilted and moved too quickly. Breckin was there in an instant, grabbing the ropes tightly and stopping our descent. Wordlessly, hand over hand, we moved down, and down, and down. We were beneath the lake; we had to be. I began to tremble with fear. What would happen when we opened the dumbwaiter door? Would the water rush in and drown us?

At last the dumbwaiter stopped with a *thump*. We had landed somewhere, on some hard surface. I wrapped my arms around myself to stop my shivering, and Breckin rubbed my shoulders hard. Then he reached for the bronze knob on the door, ready to open it.

"Wait!" I cried. He stopped and looked at me. I could think of no reason to stop him, though, and he turned back to the door and pushed it open.

Chapter 8

In Which I Dance

I could not believe what I saw. There was no water, not even a hint of the fact that we must be below the lake. Instead a path stretched forward before us, lit with a silvery light that might have been the moon, if we had not been beneath a lake. Trees lined the path, trees of silver. They cast shadows on the ground, clear enough to see each branch and leaf etched in light. A gentle breeze played among them, making the leaves knock together with a sound like the wind chimes that Cook liked to hang in her kitchen garden. I caught my breath in wonder, and Breckin took my hand and squeezed it.

I reached up with my free hand to feel a leaf, and it was cold and metallic. Quickly I pulled out the knife from my bundle and sliced off the leaf. It came away in my hand, and I held it up to see it better.

"It *is* silver," Breckin said, awed. "Silver trees. Where *are* we?"

A movement caught my eye, and I saw one of my sisters in the distance, hurrying along the path. "Come!" I cried. "We can't lose them!" We began to run, but my sisters moved quickly too, and we could not catch up to them.

Before long the forest changed. Now the trees seemed to be golden, and the sound their leaves made rustling together was that of bells. We were running now, too fast to stop and pick a leaf, but I felt strange and frightened for a reason that I could not name, and I slowed enough to look behind me. What I saw made me cry out in terror. There was no path there at all, no gold or silver trees. The path seemed to be rolling up behind us, rolling as fast as we were running. Or was it faster? And what was behind it? I could smell water, and I imagined a great wall of water rushing toward us. Breckin pulled me forward, panting, "Faster! Faster!"

On we rushed, just ahead of the water and the disappearing path, and the trees changed to diamonds, so bright and many-faceted that I could hardly look at them straight on. The sound their leaves made was of harps, and it was so beautiful that I wanted to stop and listen. I slowed again for a moment, but Breckin pulled me on. At last we came to the edge of the diamond forest, and there before us was a castle, with turrets flying flags that I could not make out. From the castle we could hear the sounds of music, and we raced to the drawbridge, which was down. Across it we flew, and it snapped up just behind us. We stopped, panting, waiting for the sound of the wall of water that had followed us crashing against the door, but heard nothing except the strains of lovely music wafting from within.

Wild-eyed, we looked at each other. "What . . . ?" Breckin whispered, and I shook my head. I had no idea what had just happened. It made no sense to me.

We stood for a moment to catch our breath. Then we started toward the music. Torches lit the marble hallway we were in, and rich, intricate tapestries lined the walls. They were embroidered with animals I had only heard of in stories—unicorns with single ivory horns, and horses with huge satiny wings, and birdlike animals with lions' manes. The air smelled perfumed, with food and flowers both, and I inhaled deeply, smelling buttery pastry and roses, wine and cardamom and lilies.

The music drew us on to the ballroom, and we stopped at the entrance to stare. The room was enormous, brightly lit with tapers and chandeliers holding long candles. Its marble floor gleamed between dancing couples, and at the far end, on a dais, an orchestra played. Twelve pairs stepped to each other, then back, whirled and spun with abandon. My sisters were the dancers, and each of them, from Aurelia to Anisa, was partnered with a princely-looking young man. The men were tall, handsome, and dressed in the richest of fabrics, and all their heads sported royal diadems. They knew all the steps perfectly, and their bows and turns were graceful in the extreme. My hands flew to my cheeks in shock as I watched my sisters clasp hands with these strangers, spin around, curtsy and twirl and clasp hands again.

"Oh my," I said faintly.

"Step back, Zita!" Breckin warned me in a low voice. "We can't be seen."

No one seemed to be paying attention to us, but I stepped back from the doorway and peered back in. I could see a long table laden with the most wonderful-looking food: piles of profiteroles and jewel-like candies, cakes and tarts decorated with sugar flowers, sugarplums and bowls of toffee, punchbowls filled with mulled wine. It made me dizzy just to look at it, and I realized all at once that I was starving. I began to move into the room and toward the table, almost as if in a trance. Breckin was after me in an instant.

"Stop!" he hissed. "Don't you know about enchanted food?"

"No," I said crossly, awakened from my sudden hunger and rubbing my arm where he had pulled me. "How could I know about it? We were never taught about magic."

"If you eat enchanted food, you become part of the enchantment, or so they say," he told me. "Remember the chocolate?"

I nodded, tearing my eyes away from the bounty on the table. I looked toward my sisters on the dance floor. "Why don't they see us?" I asked.

"I don't know," Breckin said. "Maybe it's part of the magic. Or maybe they are too intent on their partners. We must be careful when the song ends."

But the song did not end, or it became a new song without stopping. On and on the dancers danced, and we watched as the hours passed, our mouths watering from the scents of the enchanted food.

At one point we moved onto the dance floor and began to dance. I could not say why we did it; it was as if we were pulled there. We concentrated very hard on becoming like princes and princesses, using the skill that Babette had taught us, and I could see in the mirrors that lined one wall that we were interchangeable with the other couples there. At first it was wonderful:

we twirled and spun on the slippery marble floor, and the music seemed to fill me with a great energy and happiness. I had never had a chance to use the dance steps that my sisters had taught me, and I had never danced in any other arms but theirs. It was wonderful. But soon I noticed that I was no longer dancing because I wanted to. Instead, somehow, I felt compelled to dance; I tried to stop but could not. Our whirling motion was taking us closer and closer to the other dancers, and my concentration was starting to wane. I feared that if we came too near, someone would surely notice us. Frantic, I raised my eyes to Breckin and found the same panic reflected in his face. With all our strength, we aimed ourselves back toward the entryway, and when we were through the doorway and out of sight of the ballroom we staggered to a stop, breathing raggedly.

"What was that?" I asked, bewildered. "I couldn't stop!"

"No," panted Breckin, "and I'd bet they can't, either." We looked again into the ballroom, and I saw my sisters whirling about, their dresses fanning out in a circle as they spun. Now I noticed their faces, and I felt a pang, for they looked sick with exhaustion, ready to drop. They were not enjoying their night of dancing; they were being forced to dance on, and on, and on, just as we had been. They did not stumble, nor even slow, but

I got the impression that they would have fallen flat if magic had not kept them upright.

"Oh, we must do something!" I whispered, horrified. "It will kill them!"

"What would you do?" Breckin asked me. "We daren't."

I set my jaw stubbornly. "I'll just step out and shout. That will stop the music. Then they'll have to stop dancing."

"You can't!" Breckin protested. "What if something terrible happened to them? We have no power here, no weapons—nothing! We must tell Babette and get her advice. We have no idea what to do here."

I sank to the floor, my eyes filling with tears. Adena and Asmita were ill, perhaps dying, and the others would follow them soon if this kept up. How much longer could they dance? Breckin, distressed, patted my arm, but I only cried harder. He knelt beside me and held me, and I snuffled into his shoulder, shuddering with my sobs.

"We'll save them," he whispered, stroking my hair. I relaxed into his arms, and my sobs died away. For a time we stayed there, the cold marble floor hard beneath us. Then I wiped my eyes and watched the dance again. The night seemed to be taking forever, and I could hardly believe the dancers could keep on. They danced gavottes, in which the men and women met and twirled and separated again, and waltzes, in which pairs whirled up and down the floor held tightly together. They paraded through upheld arms in country dances, and kicked high in the saltarello. As my sisters twirled around their kneeling partners in a pavane, I looked at the princes to see whether they seemed tired. They were all so handsome, and all different—one with dark curls and flashing eyes, another with brown wavy hair and dimples. I looked hard at the prince dancing with Allegra, for there was something familiar about him. Could I have met him before? No, that wasn't it. He was very tall, with dark hair, and his teeth flashed white as he smiled, and I noticed that his hands, as he reached upward to clasp Allegra's hands, were exceeding long and graceful. Suddenly I remembered a Sunday evening I had spent with my sisters in which they had described the men they would like to meet and marry. It was just a game among girls, we lying on the beds, giggling and blushing in the dark. It did not seem so funny now. I recalled that Allegra's description was of a tall man, with long dark hair, the whitest teeth, and the hands of an artist.

I searched my mind for the descriptions the others had given that night. Aurelia had wanted a military man, I remembered her saying with a laugh, "so he can keep the kingdom safe while I rule." Her dance partner wore boots, a sash, military ribbons, and medals. Althea had longed for a poet, with long red curls and dreamy eyes, and that was who she danced with. I looked from one sister's partner to the next and realized it was true: each sister danced with the man of her secret longings.

I couldn't bear to watch any longer. I covered my eyes with my hands and tried to rest, but the music was relentless, its beauty now a torment rather than a pleasure. I tried to cover my ears instead, but the music seeped through. My head pounded. Long hours seemed to pass this way. Then I heard a noise over the music.

"Was that—"

"That sounded like—," Breckin and I said together. It sounded again, and this time I could tell it was a rooster's call. Day was coming.

At once the orchestra ceased to play, and we stood and moved to look into the ballroom. As we watched, wide-eyed, the couples separated, and the princes bowed in unison. My sisters curtsied, their grace belying their exhaustion. As one, the princes turned and walked to a doorway I hadn't noticed, behind the orchestra's dais. In a moment they were gone. The musicians followed them. The torches extinguished themselves. The tables of food wavered in the dim near-daylight coming in through the tall French windows, and then they too disappeared.

My sisters stood for a minute, heads bowed, but then they picked up their skirts and began hurrying to the entryway. Galvanized, Breckin and I turned and ran down the hall, fearful that they would notice us. As we reached the inner door, it opened, and the drawbridge lowered itself. We dashed across and hid behind a jeweled tree as the princesses hurried across and onto the path.

"We must get back before they do!" I whispered. "If I'm not in bed when they arrive . . ."

We couldn't stay on the path in front of them; they would surely see us. So we began to run beside the path, darting among the trees. We discovered, though, that the meager light that illuminated the path did not extend to the forest. Even a step off the path plunged us into utter darkness. I stumbled into a tree, feeling the touch of the diamond leaves like little knives on my face.

"Babette's light!" Breckin hissed, and I reached into my pocket and brought it out. I thought *light* at it, concentrating, and it began to glow with just enough light to guide us. We ran fast, and soon passed my sisters, for they were moving less quickly now than they had on the way there, their tattered shoes and tired legs slowing them. I wondered whether the path was rolling up behind them, and the water coming on behind the path, but I could not spare the time to worry. Through the diamond trees, and then through the gold, and finally through the silver we sped. We broke out of the trees then and back onto the path, and I jammed the light-stick back in my pocket. There in front of us was the dumbwaiter, its door ajar and waiting. We tumbled in and began to work the ropes frantically. Up and up we rose as we grunted and groaned with the effort. As we passed the kitchen, Breckin tumbled out, and I kept going alone, up through the sleeping palace until I reached the bedchamber closet. I sprang out, then began lowering the dumbwaiter as fast as I could. It went down and down, much farther than it should have, and at last I felt it thump to a stop far below. A moment later, I could see the ropes begin to work again, and I knew that two of my sisters were coming up. I stripped off my clothes, ran to Asmita's bed, and tossed them underneath. Then I pulled on my nightdress and jumped into bed, pulling up the bedclothes and trying hard to calm my breathing.

I watched through half-closed eyes as they returned. First Anisa and Asmita, then Allegra and Akila, Alima and Amina, Asenka and Adena, Althea and Ariadne, and last of all, Alanna and Aurelia, all as pale as death, with great dark circles under their eyes, hair tangled, and hands trembling. They pulled off their shoes, dresses, and jewels and threw them in the closet, helped one another on with their nightclothes, and collapsed into bed. A minute later, there was no sound in the room at all except for the ragged breathing of twelve girls asleep.

Chapter 9

IN WHICH HELP IS SOUGHT

must have slept for a few hours, for when I woke the room streamed with sunlight. My sisters slept on, their forms still beneath their covers, their faces pale and quiet. I crept out of bed, careful not to disturb Asmita, and pulled my dirty, wrinkled clothing from beneath the bed. I dressed quickly and stumbled toward the closet, then changed my mind when I determined that it was late enough for the kitchen to be bustling with activity. I could not take the dumbwaiter down; I would have to chance the stairs. I opened the door cautiously and peered out. The guard sat tiredly in his chair, ignorant of all that had happened in the night. And just outside the door were my sisters' shoes, lined up two by two, tattered and worn. I stared at the shoes, then turned back and quickly tiptoed to the closet. The pile of dresses was gone, all brushed and hung neatly. Was this more magic? Was even their clothing enchanted?

Just before I closed the bedchamber door, I remembered the sponge full of chocolate I had tossed under Ariadne's bed. I dashed back and retrieved it and then snuck down the stairs, turning myself into a piece of statuary for a moment when Chiara approached with a dustcloth on the second floor, and ran into the kitchen breathlessly, ready to face Cook's wrath.

"So the slugabed has decided to join us!" Cook said, taking in my rumpled, stained appearance. "Child, you look terrible. Are you ill? And did you sleep in your clothes?"

I nodded meekly. "I was so weary, Cook. I fell asleep without undressing, and I slept late—I'm sorry."

She harrumphed. "You don't look at all rested, Zita. Are you sure you're not spoiling for an ague? A little castor oil—"

"No indeed!" I interrupted. "I feel fine. Very good, in fact. All that sleep has given me plenty of energy. I thought perhaps I could go mushrooming—it's been so damp lately."

Cook pursed her lips, frowning. "Mushrooms—this late in the year? I don't think so."

"I've seen them," I said eagerly. "Just inside the forest. A group of puffballs, and some morels, too."

"Venison with mushrooms," Cook mused. "Oh, that would be a treat. Perhaps the princesses would eat some. Very well, you go—but don't be long. And wear a warm cloak!"

"Yes, ma'am," I promised, hurrying to the cloakroom. I pulled my warmest woolen cloak off a peg and reached for a basket, reminding myself that I must somehow find mushrooms before I returned. In a moment I was over the bridge and running for the woods and Babette.

I arrived at her cottage panting and disheveled and hammered on the door wildly. She was there in an instant, opening the door so suddenly that I fell across the doorstep and sprawled in a heap on the floor.

"Zita! Child, are you all right?" Babette bent to help me up and I gripped her arms so tightly that she winced. "Come, come, sit down, my dear," she murmured soothingly as I got to my feet and stumbled to the table. A cup of tea sat steaming there, and Babette commanded me, "Drink." I lowered my head to the cup, breathing in the steam, and gradually my heart slowed a little and I could sip the hot tea without my hands trembling.

Babette closed the front door and joined me at the table. She placed her warm, wrinkled hands around mine as they clasped the teacup.

"What have you seen to frighten you so?" she asked me in a calm voice. "Tell me all that happened."

I took a deep breath. "It was as you said," I told her. "The chocolate was drugged, so I poured mine into a sponge. I didn't sleep. I saw it all." I told her of my sisters dressing, taking the dumbwaiter down and down, following them along the path, through the silver and golden and diamond trees with the wall of water coming up behind us. I described the palace and the ballroom, the food and the orchestra, the princes and the dances that whirled my sisters to exhaustion and beyond. I told her of racing back to the dumbwaiter, of my sisters' disrobing, of the clothes cleaned and pressed and hung by morning and the tattered shoes lined up two by two in the hallway. When I was finished, I laid my head down on my folded arms on the table and closed my eyes. All I wanted to do was sleep.

Babette was silent for a long time. Then she said, "It is a very strong enchantment. I wish I could learn *why*. If we knew why, we could perhaps figure out how, and then we could find out how to stop it. But I cannot think of why. Your father is not at war; no one wants his descendants dead. That is not to say that there aren't many who would like to see him suffer—your father makes enemies much more easily than he makes friends. But I have not heard of any great enmity borne by one powerful enough to do this. I can't imagine. . . ."

I sighed wearily. "Then what are we to do?"

"We shall need help," Babette said decisively. "A prince is the usual thing."

I laughed shortly. "There is no prince willing to help us," I said. "My sisters have frightened away any possible suitors with their muteness. No prince would come within a hundred leagues of us."

"Even if the usual prize were offered?" Babette said.

"The usual prize?"

"You know—the hand of the eldest princess in marriage?"

I stared at her. "For one thing, Father would never offer Aurelia to anyone that way. And even if he would, to get him to do it, we'd have to tell him that there was an enchantment. Think of how he would react to that!"

Babette thought, and grimaced. "Yes, I can see you'd not want that," she said. "But it may be unavoidable. He's going to figure it out sooner or later."

"Later, then," I said. "He is very certain that there is no magic in the kingdom. He's not likely to jump to that conclusion." We thought for a few minutes.

"What of Breckin's brother, Milek?" I suggested at

last. "He is honorable, courageous—just right for the job. And I believe he has . . . feelings for Aurelia."

"But you told me he is gone to help his mother," Babette pointed out. "We cannot say when he will be back—and I do not think we have much time."

"Then we must find a prince ourselves," I said. "But how?"

Babette pursed her lips. "We shall write to their fathers, asking for the sons' help. A courteous king will not refuse us."

"But . . ." I hesitated. "Why would they respond to a letter from us? A kitchen maid and a—" I didn't know quite what to call Babette.

"An old witch?" she suggested, smiling broadly. "No, they would not take us very seriously. We shall have to write as your father."

"Oh dear," I said, gulping.

"And that puts a lot of responsibility on you, my dear," Babette went on. "You will have to get the stationery and write the letters—how is your hand?"

"Tolerable," I said. I had practiced writing for my sisters until they approved my calligraphy.

"And you shall have to intercept the return letters so your father does not see them."

"Oh dear," I said again, faintly.

Together, we came up with a list of princes. There

were King Damon's four sons who had once danced with my sisters, the brothers Bazyli and Ade of Tem, Prince Regan from Blaire, Prince Kiros from Nara, and Prince Riane from Tybal, far to the east. They were the only names I knew, so they would have to do. We worked out a formula for my letter:

Dear [Name of Prince],

We are writing to request your help in breaking an enchantment that holds our daughters captive. The usual reward of a princess's hand in marriage is offered, though because the princesses are twelve in number, we shall allow the prince who succeeds to make his own choice of bride. We shall not describe the nature of the enchantment until you apply to us in person , but suffice it to say that there are no dragons involved. Please reply at your earliest convenience.

HRH (etc., etc., etc.)

Babette and I decided that I would bring the completed letters to her, and she would figure out how to get them to their intended audiences. I did not enquire whether she would use magic to do this or would rely on the regular horse post, but I did express my worry as to the timing.

"We must hurry," I told her. "My sisters are worsening. Their exhaustion may kill them. Will the letters arrive in time? Will the princes come in time?"

To her credit, Babette did not lie to me. "I do not know, my dear," she said softly. "We can only do our best." I nodded and stood to leave, my letter draft clutched tightly in my hand.

"You were very brave," Babette said as she hugged me. "It must have been frightening, down below the lake."

"It was . . . strange," I replied. "What was frightening was to see my sisters enchanted. The rest was—well, it was exciting. Wondrous. Beautiful and terrible both." Then I remembered something. I put my hand into my skirt pocket and pulled out the silver leaf I had cut free. I laid it on the table. It was a remarkable thing: as pliable as a real, living leaf, with veins of darker silver.

Babette picked it up and looked at it closely. Then she sighed deeply. "That is magic. Beautiful and terrible. Some is more beautiful; some is more terrible. Your sisters are trapped in the terrible, and we will get them out. Do not despair!"

"I won't," I promised, placing the leaf back in my pocket. "I won't!"

On my way back to the palace, I found a small grove with morel mushrooms still growing, poking out from the dusting of snow that covered the ground. I picked them hurriedly, and as I moved toward the lakeshore, I met Breckin, who was exercising Amina's horse. He tumbled from the saddle and ran to me.

"Have you been to see Babette?" he asked. "What did she say?"

I told him our idea, and he nodded. "We do need help," he said. "I don't have the first idea what to do to break an enchantment."

"But will the princes know?" I asked. "Are princes born knowing how to do that? Or do their fathers tell them when they reach eighteen? And will they even come? Surely they all know of my father. They'll be unlikely to want to brave his wrath."

"But they will think it is he who wrote to them," Breckin pointed out. "They will think the king would be grateful to them. I believe they will come."

"I hope you are right," I said fervently. We made a plan then: I would write out the letters and leave them in a packet in the stable, and Breckin would make sure they got to Babette. We clasped hands to say good-bye, and I ran across the bridge, swinging my basket full of mushrooms for Cook to make into a dish tempting enough to convince my sisters to eat.

That evening, when I was certain my father was dining well on venison and morels, I snuck into his private rooms. I tiptoed past the outer chamber and into his study. His long mahogany desk stood in shadows, covered with papers and quills. I crept up to it, my eyes searching frantically for paper with the royal crest. There! I scooped up a sheaf of thick, cream-colored paper with Father's blue and gold crest on the top. Then I noticed the wax stick and the Great Seal, and my heart sank. I had forgotten that for a missive from Father to be official, it had to be sealed with wax with the impression of the Great Seal pressed into it.

Suddenly I heard a noise at the outer door. I turned frantically and saw the deep-blue velvet drapes at the long windows. They pooled on the floor, and I could tell that with their weight and length, I could hide behind them and not be seen. I pushed the sheaf of paper into my deep apron pocket and darted between drape and window, shivering when I felt the chill of the night beyond the window. For good measure, I used Babette's trick and tried to become the curtains. I heard footsteps enter the study, then proceed onward to the closet. Fearfully I peeked out and saw my father, shaking out a velvet jacket. I drew in a long, trembling breath: Father must have gotten chilly in the dining room and come in for a warm jacket. I tried not to move, but Father's ears were keen, and he stopped in his tracks.

"Who is there?" he called sharply.

I knew I was found out. "It is I, your Majesty," I said, coming out from behind the drapes. "I am sorry. I didn't mean to trespass. I was"—my mind raced frantically—"looking for a book."

"A book?" Father's eyebrows drew together. "Do you read, then?"

"Well, yes," I improvised. "I started on cookbooks, of course. But I have become very interested in"—I cast my eye quickly over the nearest bookcase—"in poetry."

To my surprise, Father did not grow angry or dismiss me. Instead he walked over to the bookcase. He put his hand on a volume, bound in rich plum-colored leather, and gently pulled it free.

"Your mother loved poetry," he said softly. "That is how I wooed her. I wrote her love poems cribbed from this book."

"You mean you said the poems were yours?" I couldn't help myself; it was too strange and shocking.

He nodded, and I saw the ghost of a smile tremble at his lips. He seemed almost to be in a dream.

"She knew they were not mine, of course," he said. "But she did not tell me until after we were wed. How she laughed at me!" His voice was filled with a terrible yearning, and I felt my heart contract with pity. I stepped forward.

"Oh, Father," I said, and touched his arm.

My touch woke him from his reverie, and he turned to look at me, the familiar scowl back in place.

"You should be at your tasks, child, not dallying in here," he reprimanded me, though his voice was not as harsh as usual. I scurried to the door, turning to curtsy.

"Wait," he said. He came forward, and held out the book in his hand to me.

"It was her favorite," he said roughly. For a moment I wasn't sure what to do. Then I realized he was giving me the book, and I reached out and took it, my hand shaking.

"Now go!" Father commanded, and I fled.

That night, before I began to write my pleading letters to the princes on the paper I had stolen, I looked through the book of poems. I had not really ever read poetry before. Poetry was not encouraged in my sisters' education, so they had not passed it on to me. At first I could hardly bear to open the volume, knowing my mother's hands had once held it. I stroked the smooth leather and looked at the title, embossed in gold. *Poems of Longing, Love, and Loss.* When I looked inside it at last, it fell open to one page, and I read:

I ne'er was struck before that hour
With love so sudden and so sweet,
Her face it bloomed like a sweet flower
And stole my heart away complete.

I liked the sweet sound of it, the rhymes and rhythm of the lines. I tried to picture my father writing these words, passing them off as his own, and my mother reading them, laughing, knowing he'd lied. Could Father really have once been that besotted young man? It seemed incredible to me.

I let the book fall open again and read:

Now folds the lily all her sweetness up,
And slips into the bosom of the lake:
So fold thyself, my dearest, thou, and slip
Into my bosom and be lost in me.

I felt a heat rise to my face as I read the poem, and closed my eyes quickly. I wasn't sure what it meant, but the words spoke so strongly that I was embarrassed without quite knowing why. Quickly I thumbed through the pages again, and they opened to a third poem:

The dew falls thick, my blood grows cold.
Draw, draw the closèd curtains: and make room:
My dear, my dearest dust; I come, I come.

I closed the book again, tears flooding my eyes. *My dearest dust; I come, I come.* Oh, poor Father! If that was how my mother's death made him feel, how could he bear it?

I tucked the small volume away in the box of treasures beneath my bed and turned to the task of writing to the princes. I was too tired to work well, though, and spoiled the first two letters with blots. Determined, I tried again. This time my hand was steadier, and the letters came out tolerably well—not quite the work of a royal scribe, to be sure, but passable. When the ink had dried, I folded them and hid them. It was nearly dawn, and I knew the palace would soon be stirring. I would have to wait until evening to stamp the letters with the royal seal. I fell into bed, but even weary as I was, sleep did not come at once; when I closed my eyes, I saw again my sisters' whirling dance and heard the strains of the violins. Such beautiful music! Such beautiful, beautiful music.

The sun had long been up when I woke, and I cursed myself for wasting time that I could have spent in helping my sisters. Quickly I dressed and washed and hurried down to the kitchen, where I found Cook alone stirring a pot of broth.

"Another princess ailing," she reported to me. "Ariadne it is, this time. I'm to make a restorative broth for them all, says the doctor. Fool!"

"Why a fool?" I asked sharply, taking the spoon from her hand and stirring. After the hours I had spent wondering who had woven my sisters' enchantment, everyone seemed a possible witch or wizard—even Cook. For how could Cook know that broth would fail, unless she . . .

"Has anything that man tried done the least bit of good?" Cook demanded. "Have those girls not gone downhill since the day Dr. Idiot set foot in this palace? How *not* a fool, I ask you? Restorative broth, indeed!"

"What would you do for them?" I asked her, pushing down my mistrust with an effort. Cook was no witch. She was a dear, sensible soul who would always do what she could for my sisters. Dr. Valentin, on the other hand . . . Was it true that my sisters had worsened ever since he first came? But Adena was ill before that. Oh, the endless suspicion made my head spin!

"They need rest," Cook said definitively. "Do you know that they are walking through their shoes each night? Our cobblers aren't able to keep up with repairing them! I don't know what's gotten into the princesses, or why they walk, but walk they do, and they must stop. The guard your father has put on their door has done no good at all! You know, gossip says—" She stopped herself, looking abashed.

"Gossip says what?" I demanded.

"No offense meant," Cook said, a little shamefaced, "but you should probably know that people think they are out looking for husbands."

I gave a hoot of laughter. "Walking through their shoes every night looking for husbands? I've never heard anything so ridiculous!"

Cook nodded emphatically. "It is ridiculous, and I gave those gossips the right side of my rolling pin for it! But still . . ."

"Still . . . ," I echoed, and then the kitchen was silent, except for the crackling of the ever-present hearth fire and the sound of the spoon moving through the broth, round and round.

In the quiet time between luncheon and preparing for dinner, I escaped to my room and stuffed the letters into my apron pocket. Later, when Father was at dinner again, I snuck into his study and lit a candle from the embers in the fireplace. Then I used the candle to melt wax from the wax stick onto each of the letters. With my heart pounding, I picked up the Great Seal and pressed it into each wax dripping. There!

As the wax dried, I admired my work, too engrossed in my success to notice the odd flickering of the candle that I had placed on the desk. Then, suddenly, there was a puff of breath from behind me, and the candle was out. I squawked like a surprised chicken and turned, trying to adjust my eyes to the sudden dimness of the room.

Standing there was my father, his anger making him

seem even taller and more formidable than usual. The man from the night before, who had spoken tenderly of poetry and of my mother, was nowhere in his visage. I shrank backward, but there was no escaping.

"Are you looking for more poems to read?" he asked sarcastically. I was too frightened to reply.

"Give those to me," he demanded, pointing to the letters. His voice was deceptively soft. I was powerless to disobey. Shaking, I picked up the letters and handed them to him. He pulled one letter open and read it, squinting in the dim light, then strode to the fireplace with the bunch of them and tossed them in. The flames leaped up, happy to have something as tasty as paper to eat, and in a moment my work was consumed.

Father turned back to me. His brows were lowered and his eyes flashed. "You would make us a laughing-stock," he said to me, his voice still low. "You would write this—this *ridiculous*, this *absurd* letter to princes across the land, in my name. In *my name!*" Now his voice was getting louder, and I shrank back still more.

"But your Majesty—," I tried.

"You would tell them there is an enchantment here, when all know that magic has been banned from this kingdom?"

I scrambled away from him, trying to explain, but he overrode my feeble voice with his roar.

"You would make me look powerless to help my own daughters? You would invite the sons of the king of Tem, the son of the king of Nara here? *You would do that?*" And now his fury was full force, and I sank to the floor weeping, apologizing, telling him that I was wrong, I shouldn't have done it, I would never do anything like that again.

It was shameful, I know, the cowardly way I behaved, but it wasn't just that I was afraid. It was that I didn't want to hurt him. I didn't want him to think that I had meant to make him a laughingstock. I didn't want to lose his love. And wasn't that the ridiculous thing, the absurd thing? Because I knew full well that I had never had his love to lose.

Chapter 10

In Which Help Arrives

 snuck out that night, dodging past the guard as he dozed and crossing the bridge that was now slick with snow. I found Breckin asleep in the stables and woke him to tell him of the failure of our plan.

"You must go to Babette and explain what happened," I instructed. "I cannot do it myself. I have the strangest feeling—like someone is watching me. I do not want to lead them to Babette." I felt a little silly saying this to Breckin, but he took me seriously.

"Your father is angry and suspicious," he reminded me. "If he thinks you are set on sending these letters, he's probably set someone to watch and make sure you don't write them again and send them. Have you actually seen anyone?"

"No," I admitted. "I look behind myself a hundred times a day, and there's no one there, but I could swear I feel eyes on me."

"Just go about your business," Breckin said, "and I'll talk to Babette. I'm sure she has come up with other ideas."

I was not so sure, but I had no choice but to return to my rounds of cleaning and cooking, dusting and baking.

As the next few days passed and I waited anxiously for Breckin to contact me, I knew that my sisters continued their nightly pilgrimage beneath the lake. Their shoes appeared each morning, worn and tattered, and one by one they fell ill, keeping to their beds, until Father dined alone at the long table each night while his daughters languished upstairs. At midnight I listened for the sound of the dumbwaiter descending and wept as it passed by the pantry, carrying the girls to their nightly dance. It was a torment to me, this doing nothing. I could not sleep; I had trouble eating. The circles under my eyes rivaled Aurelia's.

I spent still more time trying to figure out who was behind the enchantment. I looked at everyone with suspicion, from the maids who were my friends to the footmen, Burle, and Chiara. I knew I had no real reason to suspect Burle except that I did not like him, but Chiara in particular caught my attention, with her perpetually sour expression and brusque manner. I remembered that she had called my sisters "spoiled" after one of the disastrous dinners with the princes. And I recalled seeing her the night that I had noticed the princesses' shoes in the hallway. I told myself that it was not unusual for her to be at her work at that hour, but still I wondered. Determined to find out what I could, I followed her around, trying to keep from being seen. Her eyes were sharp, though, accustomed as she was to noticing the smallest object undusted or out of place, and when I shadowed her to the dining room and she turned and tripped over me, at last she grew annoyed.

"Zita, get out from underfoot!" she scolded me. "Attend to your work, child, and let me do mine." Her voice was rough, and I scurried back belowstairs, more uncertain than ever.

My sisters' door was barred to me now, and still I felt eyes upon me as I passed through the long hallways and up the marble staircases of the palace. I had begun to realize that there was magic in the watching, and I remembered that Cook had once told me that Father watched me. I suddenly wondered if they were Father's eyes on me. The implications of that were terrible: if Father was watching me, and the watcher was the one who had enchanted my sisters, then . , . I tried to shrug off the thought, but it would not leave me.

On a Tuesday morning a week after Father had burned my letters, I pulled down my apron from the hook on which it hung in the kitchen cloakroom. When I tied it on, I heard something crackle in the pocket, and I pulled out a piece of brown packaging paper, scrawled with writing. I scanned the signature and saw it was from Breckin. The writing was rough, but I was pleased at the content. *Come to the stables tonight if you can,* it said. *I have something I must show you. B.*

For the first time in days, I felt a little pinch of hope. Perhaps Breckin and Babette had a new plan or had discovered something important. Perhaps there would be something for me to *do*. But to get safely to the stables I had to escape the eyes that I knew were constantly on me, tracking my every move. I experimented with Babette's trick and found that if I became something else, I lost the feeling of being watched. That worked when I was still—if I became like a hat stand, for instance, or a pillar. The moment I moved, though, I again felt that scrutiny. I tried another experiment before dinner. When all the serving girls traipsed down the stairs to the kitchen, I mingled with them and used my trick to become one of them. And the watched feeling disappeared.

After dinner and the clearing up, I pulled on my cloak and became a lamppost on the land bridge. I had to concentrate very hard to keep from shivering in the cold, damp air and to stay a lamppost at the same time, but I knew I was succeeding because I felt no eyes upon me. I waited there for what seemed like hours, until a group of servants—the underbutler Burle and several footmen—came out, headed to the nearest tavern a full two miles away. I became one of them, joking and pushing with the others, until we were safely across the bridge and on the path that led through the woods. Then I peeled off from the group, hearing one of them cry, "Wait! Who is that?" as I fled through the trees toward the stables. Nobody followed me, though, and I arrived at the stables panting from my run.

Breckin waited for me outside the stable door, and he pulled me inside without speaking. The air was warm with horse smells and hay smells, punctuated by the breathy snorts and whinnies of the inhabitants. It was a cozy place, a friendly place, and I envied Breckin for being able to spend his days there.

I looked at him, and even in the darkness of the stable I could see that his face was flushed.

"What is it? What do you need to show me?" I asked him.

He pointed behind me. "This!" he said with a flourish.

I turned and gave a yelp. There was someone standing behind me. Moonlight slanted through the stable window, and in its glow I saw that it was Milek.

"I am so glad to see you!" I cried. "Oh Milek, you must help us!"

"Breckin has been telling me what has happened," Milek said, his face somber. "You cannot get a prince, so I am afraid you will have to be content with me. I've never fought against magic before, but my sword is at your service, and at your sisters'."

"Will you get in trouble for leaving your post?" Breckin asked his brother.

"A soldier fights his battles as he finds them," Milek said. "Mine is here, and now."

"If we do not do something soon, my sisters will die," I said flatly. Milek looked at me with concern. I knew he was thinking of Aurelia.

"It is that bad, then?"

"They are all bedridden now," I told him, "too weak to get up, too weak to eat more than a few sips of broth. And yet every night they dress in satin and velvet and dance until dawn. It will kill them soon." I could not voice my suspicion of my father, though I knew I should. I was wracked with guilt over thinking such a thing of him, and filled with fear that I was putting Milek and Breckin in danger by saying nothing.

"Then we must act immediately," Milek said. He reached across the hay and squeezed my hand, and tears rushed to my eyes. It seemed so unlikely that he, a single poor soldier, could help, but I felt my burden lighten just a little.

"What should we do?" I asked him, sniffling.

"I think I should meet your witch first," he said. "Find out if she has any magic that can help us or if she's learned anything new. Then we will make our plan."

We set off for Babette's, and when we arrived, the chimney was smoking merrily and the cottage was warm and filled with the smell of cinnamon buns baking. Babette had just pulled a trayful from the oven, and we all three were quiet as we chewed and swallowed in a rare moment of contentment.

"Oh, wonderful, wonderful, ma'am," Milek said at last, licking buttercream frosting off his fingers. "Only my mother can make a cinnamon bun to rival this."

A blush spread across Babette's wrinkled cheeks, and I suddenly saw how she might have looked when she was a great deal younger. She lowered her eyes. "Well, there's a little magic in them," she admitted. "But most of it is just baking."

"You have frosting on your nose," Breckin said to me,

and I stuck my tongue out at him and went on eating.

When we were replete, we sat back, and Babette looked hard at Milek. He was calm under her scrutiny. I could see she liked that. They held each other's gaze for a long minute, and then Babette said, "So this is our prince. I think you will do very nicely, sir."

Milek inclined his head and replied, "Thank you, ma'am. I will surely try my best."

Babette turned to me. "You say there is a guard outside the princesses' door?"

I nodded.

"And he has failed in his office, of course. The princesses are still ruining their shoes each night. So there will be a new guard needed. Who better for the job than this brave soldier, lately returned from the Reaches and eager for a new position?"

I clapped my hands. "Oh, very good! Breckin can introduce him to Burle, the underbutler. I am sure he will give Milek the post. He will have access to my sisters then. But . . . what next?"

"You will have to go back below the lake, and Milek will go with you. I think the way will be made clear to you then." She turned to Milek. "You must follow your heart, young man. Even if it seems that your heart is telling you to do the most foolish thing, do it."

Milek smiled. "My heart has not been foolish for

these twenty-seven years," he said. "I do not think it will start now."

Babette's eyes twinkled, but she did not reply. Then she turned to me again. "My dear," she said, "you have said you think you are being watched by someone. I think it is the magician who has enchanted your sisters." I nodded but said nothing, hoping she could not read my thoughts. "You must be very careful. Do not be seen with Milek, or with Breckin if you can help it. Remember that if you go with your sisters to the dance, the eyes will be on you."

"But I can trick them!" I said excitedly. "I have come and gone freely by fooling the watcher into thinking I am something else."

"That may not always work," Babette warned. "If the witch or wizard figures out what you are doing, you will be exposed. Be careful. All three of you, please be careful!"

Before we parted, Babette brought out a dark cloak made from a cloth I could not identify. In fact, though I stared hard at it, I could not tell what color it was. Perhaps the brown of autumn leaves, but in a slant of sunlight it looked greenish, and the flickering firelight showed glints of gold.

"For you," she said to Milek, and draped the cloak around his shoulders. "It was once a cloak of invisibility, though most of that magic has worn off. Get your brother to teach you to become other than you are, and this cloak will help you create the illusion. You will not have days to practice as these two have had, so the cloak will give you an extra edge. You will need it."

Milek bowed, and the cloak billowed around him. "I thank you, ma'am," he said. "I hope your faith in me will not prove to be misplaced."

"Oh, I think it will not," Babette said, smiling. "I am a rather mediocre magician, but I am a very good judge of people."

We took our leave and walked together through the forest, dodging low-hanging branches heavy with snow. Milek looked back at the cottage and whistled through his teeth to see it in its ruined state. Before we came out of the trees, we taught Milek the art of becoming other, and with the help of his cloak, he soon was able to disappear as well as either of us. We parted company, agreeing to meet again the first night after Milek had secured his new post as the princesses' guard, and to follow my sisters that night beneath the lake.

For three nights I crept up to the long hallway at the top of the palace to see who stood before the bedroom door. For the first two nights, the guard was the hapless soul who had been sitting there for weeks as my sisters danced themselves nearly to death. On the third night, the guard was Milek. Unlike the other guard, he saw me, but he gave no sign that he knew me. I was relieved, for I knew the eyes were always on me in those days.

Burle stayed by the kitchen fire for hours that evening, drinking hard cider and annoying Salina and Bethea with his attentions. I feared he'd never leave. By eleven, though, the girls had escaped to bed and, much to my relief, Burle had left as well. At nearly midnight, I was busy being a broom in the kitchen to escape the watcher when Breckin came in, walking right past me into the pantry. For an instant I became myself again so he could see me, and then—fast enough, I hoped, to fool the ever-watchful eyes—I was a sack of flour in the pantry beside him. Milek arrived not long after, swathed in his cloak. As the clock struck, we heard the dumbwaiter begin its nightly journeys up and down. Six times in all, and then we pulled the dumbwaiter back up and jumped in quickly, squeezing in as tightly as possible. The little cupboard was a tight fit for three, and I winced at the squeaks and moans the cables let out under our weight. Milek was strong enough to control its movement downward, but I could see the strain of it in his face and in the muscles in his arms as he brought us safely to the bottom.

"Getting up will be a trick!" he whispered as we piled out and began running up the tree-lined path. The light was as odd as it had been the first night, and the trees of silver, then gold as strange and beautiful. This time I did not look back, but Milek did, and when he gasped I knew he had seen the wall of water that followed us as the path rolled up behind.

"Keep moving!" I told him, and he did, casting awed glances at the diamond forest that we now raced past.

We reached the castle in time to cross the drawbridge and heaved a collective sigh of relief as the heavy doors slammed behind us. In his rough uniform and beard, Milek looked as out of place in this realm of elegance as Breckin and I, but he showed no discomfort as we walked quickly along the empty corridors, our heels ringing on the marble floors. He paused to stare at the tapestries with their odd scenes and mythic beasts, but Breckin urged him on until we reached the ballroom. From the doorway we peered in. The same sight as before met our eyes: beautiful princesses dancing with handsome men, the orchestra playing and playing its ethereal music, the long tables laden with food that set our mouths watering.

I glanced at Milek to see if he was tempted by the food, but he was staring out at the dance floor. I followed his gaze to the form of my sister Aurelia, dressed in deepest blue velvet that matched her starry eyes. Her hair was piled atop her head, escaping in delicate wisps that framed her lovely face to great advantage. From this distance, you could not see the lack of sleep and food that drew her skin tight across her cheekbones and shadowed her eyes. She twirled in the arms of her soldier, his uniform putting Milek's shabby one to shame with its rows upon rows of medals, its sashes and saber. I looked at Milek again, ready with a wry comparison, but he was enrapt.

"What shall we do?" Breckin whispered. "Should we step out, let them know we are here?"

Brought back to himself, Milek shook his head slowly. "I don't think so," he said. "I think we must just watch."

"But we have already done that!" I cried. "What good will it do just to watch?"

Milek put his finger over his lips to hush me, and reluctantly I moved back into the hallway to watch and wait.

The evening progressed in exactly the same way as the previous one, only this time we did not make the mistake of trying to dance to the music. We explained to Milek what had happened when we did. He was fascinated by everything and looked and listened avidly, as if he were memorizing it all. He even stepped into the ballroom once or twice, with his cloak wrapped around him; the dancers took no heed of him at all. When at last the cock crowed and the orchestra disappeared, we prepared to rush back to the dumbwaiter. We had decided that we could let the princesses go up before we did, since, because it was not Sunday, I did not have to be abed to fool them when they returned, and it was good we did. No matter how Milek and Breckin pulled, they could not raise the dumbwaiter with the three of us inside, so Milek stepped out and helped us rise to the kitchen. We then sent the dumbwaiter back down, and he pulled himself up to our level.

When Milek jumped out, I let out a breath I hadn't realized I'd been holding. "I was afraid—," I began, then stopped.

"What?" Breckin asked.

"I was afraid the dumbwaiter would not go back down after you and I got out," I admitted. He and Milek looked at me blankly, and then an expression of horror came onto their faces.

"Left down there, under the lake," Breckin said hoarsely.

I interrupted hurriedly. "But it didn't happen. We needn't worry."

Milek laughed. "I'm very glad I didn't think of that beforehand. *That* might have taken away my nerve."

"You'd best get back to your post," I advised him. "It's nearly dawn, and the household will be stirring."

He nodded. "Zita, can you be in your sisters' room this afternoon? Say, at about two o'clock?" he asked.

I clasped my hands together. "Oh, do you have an idea? Has your heart told you what to do?" I asked, excited.

Milek laughed. "I don't know if it's my heart telling me. I think more likely it's my head. But yes, I do have an idea. And it involves speaking with Aurelia. Can you open the door for me at two o'clock?"

"Yes!" I cried. "I will force my way in if I have to."

"No," he cautioned me. "Don't make a scene. We need to be quiet."

"I don't know that she'll speak to you," I told him.

"Why?" he asked. "Does she not speak to commoners?"

"Oh, it's not that," I said. "She has a great sympathy and feeling for commoners. But she has not been speaking. None of them has. They are too tired. And they do not speak to men at all. Babette believes it is part of the enchantment."

"I see," he said thoughtfully. "She does not have to speak—not right away, anyway. She just needs to listen."

I was desperate to hear more, but Milek refused to tell. He took his leave from us, and Breckin snuck out to return to the stables while I walked wearily up the stairs to my room and collapsed onto my bed.

I woke a few hours later to the sounds of the house-maids cleaning outside my door. Quickly I looked out-side to see if I could judge the time from the slant of the sun, but there was no sun this day. The lowering clouds looked snow-filled. I dressed quickly and ran down to the kitchen. The clock there read one fifteen, and I apologized to Cook for neglecting both the breakfast and the lunch preparation.

Cook sighed and ruffled my already disheveled hair. "No need, little Zita," she said sadly. "No one is eating but the servants and the king. We have not much work to do these days."

"Have you something for me to bring up to the prin-cesses?" I asked innocently.

"I thought you were not allowed up there," Cook said.

"I believe they have decided it does not much matter now," I said sadly. I could play Cook like a pianoforte.

Cook pulled me to her, and I was pressed in a hug against her warm, yeast-scented bosom. "Poor Zita!" she soothed me. "Yes, you shall bring them their broth. Do try to get them to take a few sips, at least. Perhaps they'll do it for you."

Shortly after, I carried a covered tureen on a tray up the stairs to my sisters' room. Outside the door, Milek drowsed in his chair, but I did not so much as look at him as I passed by. I knocked sharply, and Nurse opened the door.

"Zita! What are you doing here?"

"I just wanted to see my sisters, Nurse," I pleaded. "I've brought them some healing broth."

"Dearie, you know I can't let you in. Your father has left me strict instructions." Her brow creased with sympathy. "Here, my love. Hand me the broth."

I was panicked. I had to get in. I had to open the door and make sure Aurelia listened to Milek. Without warning, and with little effort, I burst into wild tears. I could hear Milek turn in his chair to look at me, and I remembered his warning: *Don't make a scene.* But what else could I do?

"Oh, dearie, dearie, come here. Put that tray down," Nurse instructed me, pulling me into the room and taking the tray from me. "Just come in and calm down. Dry your poor eyes. Say hello. Then you must leave."

I entered the room. I had not been within for many days, and now everything was changed. There was a deathly hush, broken only by the breathing of the twelve girls as they lay in their featherbeds, arms resting at their sides atop the coverlets. The air was stuffy and warm and smoky from the fire, and the room was dim, for the heavy drapes had been pulled across the windows, and little light leaked around their edges. I walked between the beds, reaching out to touch each sister's limp hand: Aurelia, Alanna, Ariadne, Althea, Adena, and Asenka down one row; Amina, Alima, Akila, Allegra, Asmita, and Anisa up the other. As I walked, I whispered low, "Don't be afraid. We will help you. Don't be afraid. Don't be afraid." I do not know whether they heard me; they did not open their eyes or move their heads or even squeeze my hand.

When I got to Anisa's bed and the door, I stopped, pulled out a handkerchief, and dramatically wiped my eyes and blew my nose. At the same time, I reached out with my other hand and turned the lock on the door so that it was unlocked. The noise of my nose-blowing covered up the click of the lock turning. I did not know whether Nurse would check the door when she left the room. It was a chance I had to take.

I left the room, hurrying past Milek again without looking at him. As I went, though, I hissed, "Wait until Nurse leaves," hoping desperately that whatever watched me did not listen as well.

I must admit that I was desperate to find out what Milek planned to do. I imagined him bursting into the room, sword drawn, and challenging the magician who had entrapped my sisters. I paced up and down the stairs all afternoon, hoping that at any minute Nurse would leave. It wasn't until darkness had fallen that I finally saw her heading down to the kitchen, carrying the tray with the soup tureen. It looked as heavy as when I had brought it up. The princesses had not eaten a thing.

I ran down to the kitchen myself and hurried into the pantry. I had never used the dumbwaiter during the day before, and I knew it was a danger, but I had to know what Milek was going to do. Taking precautions that no one was near and no magical eyes were on me, I climbed on board and hoisted myself up to the bedroom closet. Then I tiptoed out and made my way down the silent rows of beds until I got to Aurelia's, near the door. I perched on the side of the bed. Aurelia gave no sign that she knew I was there, but I picked up her hand and held it, willing life and liveliness back into her. Then I heard the bedroom door click open.

I held my breath, waiting for Milek to enter, but he did not. Instead I heard his voice from the other side of the door.

"Princess Aurelia, can you hear me?"

Of course there was no answer.

"Princess Aurelia, I do not wish to disturb you or to offend you," Milek's low, gentle voice went on. "But I have had the most remarkable dream, and I wanted to tell it to you. It was a beautiful and a terrifying dream, and you were in it. Will you listen?"

Again, there was no answer, and Aurelia's hand lay lifeless in mine.

"In my dream," Milek said, "we were beneath the lake. I know that seems impossible, and in fact it was impossible, but it was a dream, was it not? So anything could happen.

"You and your sisters walked quickly along a straight path, lined with trees. You were all so very lovely. You wore a dress of midnight-blue velvet, embroidered with moonflowers along the bottom. Your earrings and necklace were sapphires, the color of your eyes. The path we walked was no ordinary path. The trees that lined it were made of silver, and the sound they created when they hit against one another in the breeze was of wind chimes."

Milek's voice had become melodious, almost a sing-song. I closed my eyes, and it was as though I were there again, beneath the lake, only now I had the time to look about me and see the extraordinary things that I'd had to race past. As he described them, I could see it all: A plumed bird sat in one of the golden trees, and its multicolored tail feathers hung down nearly to the ground. The diamond leaves caught the mysterious light that came onto the path and the reflection of the princesses' deep-colored gowns to create rainbow prisms. In the moat below the drawbridge to the castle, enormous fish broke the surface of the water, and their mouths made the shapes of words that could not be heard. The mythical beasts in the tapestries that lined the halls of the castle moved when looked at from an angle. And the princes who danced without stopping in the ballroom cast no shadows as they spun about the floor.

"The most beautiful thing I have ever seen was you, Princess Aurelia, that night in my dream," Milek said. "You stepped up to me on the dance floor, and I took you in my arms, and though it was a dream you felt real and substantial to me. You danced with such lightness, like a feather, or an angel, and your golden hair brushed my neck."

I froze as, in my hand, I felt Aurelia's fingers stir.

"We twirled about the floor for what must have been hours, but it felt like no time at all had passed. I wanted to hold you forever. I would gladly have danced with you until I died. But in my dream, the cock crowed, and I had to drop your hand and go."

Aurelia closed her fingers around my hand, as if it were her dance partner's hand and she did not want the dance to end.

"I left, and my last sight of you was your beautiful face, your sad eyes, as you picked up your skirts and hurried away. I wept for hours. I weep still. I feel that I have lost the only thing worth having." In Milek's voice,

I could hear the weeping that he described.

There was silence then, and I opened my eyes and stole a look at Aurelia. To my shock, her eyes were open wide and swimming with tears.

"Speak to him!" I urged her, though I did not know why. But she shook her head, and the tears ran down her white cheeks.

"It's all right," I soothed her. I did not know what had just happened, but it seemed to me that it was something important. Nobody had been able to bring my sisters out of their trancelike sleep for days. I looked around me and saw that each girl's eyes were open. Even as I watched, they began to drowse again, and in a few minutes all were asleep once more. Aurelia was the last to drop off, and I could see a silent plea in her face as she faded.

"Stay awake!" I begged her. It was no use; the enchantment was too strong. But they had wakened, and I knew now that they could be wakened. And perhaps, perhaps, perhaps this meant that they could be saved.

Chapter 11

In Which the Great Wave Breaks

went through the rest of day feeling, for the first time in as long as I could remember, as if something good might happen. I smiled as I did my work, and Cook and Nurse and the others smiled back at me. When I imagined my sisters asleep upstairs, I pictured their sleep as lighter, less oppressive, and I knew it was true.

Breckin, Milek, and I had made no arrangements to meet that night, but at midnight we were all together in the pantry, and again we followed my sisters to their dance, waited for them, and followed them back. This time I tried to pay attention to what I passed, and the next day, when Milek again described his "dream" to Aurelia, I could well remember the strange squirrel-like animal that leaped from golden tree to golden tree and the Turkish delight that jiggled in its silver serving dish as the dancers twirled past the groaning sideboard. I remembered Aurelia's beautiful yellow silk gown, embroidered with lavender flowers and green leaves, and her lavender satin shoes as they peeked out from beneath her skirts. I remembered the songs the musicians played, songs I had never heard before, that made my heart swell and my knees feel weak with their sweetness. Again Aurelia's eyes and the eyes of the others were open at the end of the telling, again she squeezed my hand and wept, and again she could not speak and soon drifted back to sleep. But she had been awake longer.

That afternoon I snuck out to the stables and found Breckin there, grooming a horse with long, steady strokes. The mare whinnied gently as I approached, and Breckin straightened from his task, smiling.

"Did he tell his dream again?" Breckin asked, and I nodded. "With good results?"

"I think so," I said. "They were awake a little longer. Still, if this is to work the way we're doing it, it will take weeks. Isn't there a shortcut of some sort?"

Breckin shook his head. "Milek isn't even really sure

of what he is doing," he told me. "Telling the dream was just an idea that came to him—he doesn't know what it will accomplish."

I stamped my foot, frustrated, and the mare stamped back. It made me laugh. I took the currying brush from Breckin and brushed for a little while, losing myself in the regular motion and the warmth of the horse's skin against my side as I leaned into her.

Finally I said, "I'm just worried that if we take too long, the enchanter or whoever it is will become aware. Already we are watched. It's only luck that we haven't been discovered yet."

"Luck?" Breckin cried out, startling the horse, who whinnied. "It's skill, my dear. We are apprentice witches, and soon we shall surpass our mistress. Nobody can discover us." With that, he attempted to become a broom in a tangle of brooms and brushes, but I was watching him as he did it, so it didn't really work.

"Idiot," I scoffed. "Just don't get too sure of yourself."

Breckin laughed, a little shamefaced. "I guess I'd better not," he admitted. "Don't you, either. And I'll see you tonight."

That night, trying to stay awake, I looked through the book of poetry Father had given me, reading the lines aloud. As I progressed through the volume, I found that the poems grew darker, from love to longing to loss, and the feelings they expressed more desperate. There were poems about lost love and love betrayed, false lovers and lovers who never told of their love. The language was beautiful and heartbreaking.

And then I came to a verse that made my heart stop. It was about love so strong that it caused madness. I read:

Seething pell-mell with an ominous tempest's roar.
Mad shadows, follow your desires without measure;
Never can you satisfy your rage,
And your punishment is born from your pleasure.

I read the lines over and over, trying to understand them and trying to figure out why they frightened me so. The *seething*, the *tempest's roar*—this described the wildness of my fevered dash toward the castle under the lake as the path rolled up behind me. *The mad shadows* made me think of the ghostly figures of my sisters, dancing and dancing without measure. But the *rages*, the *punishment born from pleasure*—when I read those words, I pictured my father, his mouth drawn down, his anger and his anguish. And I wondered again: could my father be doing this terrible thing to my sisters? He had banned magic, but who was to say he could not create a spell himself? Perhaps to him, it was a fitting punishment for my sisters, who lived while my mother had died. Oh, was it possible that he was completely mad? I shivered with horror at my own imagination. No, it was I who was mad even to think such a thing! I slapped the book shut and threw it beneath my bed.

I closed my eyes, trying to forget the haunting words. Before long, my sleepless nights caught up with me, and without meaning to, I drifted off. When I awoke it was late. I could hear the clock striking. Was it eleven or twelve? I couldn't be late! I leaped up as the clock struck *three, four,* and out of my room—*five, six*—stumbling down the stairs into the kitchen—*seven, eight, nine, ten.* As I dashed into the pantry I saw the dumbwaiter already beginning to descend, and I jumped inside, smashing my head and landing with a grunt on somebody within as the clock struck: *eleven, twelve.*

"Well," came Breckin's voice from very nearby. "Better late than never, I suppose."

"Sorry," I said, straightening up and trying to rearrange my skirts. "I fell asleep. These late nights . . ." I heard Milek laugh in the darkness, and then we landed with a thump. I tumbled out of the dumbwaiter and started hurrying down the path, but something stopped me in my tracks.

Eyes. Eyes on me.

I turned to Breckin and Milek in horror. When Milek

saw that I had halted, he grabbed my arm and pulled me forward. We couldn't stop. We didn't know what would happen if the path rolled up to us, if the wall of water reached us. We ran.

I tried to explain. "I didn't think to hide from the watcher," I panted. "I was half asleep. I just forgot. There's no excuse. Oh, what will happen now?"

No one answered. I had no breath to keep talking.

When at last we were inside the castle, I bent over, gasping. When I could speak again, I said to Milek, "Cover us all with your cloak. Perhaps he—they—won't see us then. Perhaps we can fool them somehow."

"I think it is too late for that," Milek said, and I knew he was right. We had been seen, and it was my fault. We were beneath the lake in an enchanted castle that could not really exist, and whoever had created the enchantment—Father? Chiara?—knew we were there.

I couldn't tell if it was my nerves or a real change, but there was a charge to the air in the ballroom this night. The music seemed faster, the dancers whirled with more abandon. It was exhausting just to watch them. As the hours ticked by, I grew more and more anxious, and I could tell that Breckin and even Milek did as well. Breckin became very twitchy and could not sit still, while Milek was so motionless that he might have been carved of stone. He did not take his eyes off Aurelia all night, and he clasped his hands together so tightly that I could see the skin marked with the imprints of his nails.

At last the waiting proved too much. Milek stood, and I held my breath as he stepped out on the dance floor and made his way through the couples to Aurelia and her prince. He tapped the prince on the shoulder, the universal signal for cutting in. Instead of turning and relinquishing his partner, the prince seemed not to feel the touch. Aurelia looked up, though, and her face changed from the entranced, expressionless visage I had always seen as she danced. A light dawned in her eyes as Milek reached out toward her again, and at that moment the rooster crowed. The orchestra dispersed and the princes made their bows as they had every night I'd watched, and then the cock crowed again, and this *cock-a-doodle-doo* was a hundred times louder than the first. Then again it crowed, louder still. My sisters froze, and the princes stopped in their tracks. The walls of the castle seemed to shake as the rooster's call came again and again, louder and louder. I clapped my hands over my ears and turned panicked eyes to Breckin.

"We must go," Breckin said. "Let's get your sisters." He walked out onto the dance floor toward his brother without hesitation. At first my sisters did not seem to see us. They stood stock-still, looking at the princes, and I looked to see what they stared at.

It was the most peculiar thing. The faces of the men wavered, as if I were looking into a mirror whose glass was uneven. As hard as I tried, I could not make out their features. As soon as I could tell the color of one prince's eyes, his mouth went out of focus, and by the time I figured out that feature, the eyes were gone. And the faces grew less and less distinguishable, until finally they had just the hint of eyes and nose and mouth and chin. As each prince became less distinct, less real, Milek, standing beside Aurelia, seemed stronger and more defined. I watched in bewilderment as the figures began to waver and shimmer, and before long the very forms of the princes were watery and unfocused. And then they were gone—just gone.

My sisters began to wail and keen, their voices barely audible above the crowing of the cock. Their faces were terrible to see, wracked with sorrow and despair, and I thought that the disappearance of the princes must somehow be the most awful, fearful thing in the world for them. My heart ached, and I stretched my arms out to Anisa, who had crumpled, weeping, to her knees.

There was a sudden loud *crash*, and abruptly the sound of the rooster stopped. Milek pointed upward, and we saw a crack had appeared in the ceiling of the ballroom. Stone and plaster rained down around us. I winced as pebbly pieces hit my head and shoulders.

"Let's go, now!" Milek shouted. He ran to Aurelia and pulled her toward the door. For a moment she resisted him, but she was exhausted and weak, and reluctantly she allowed herself to be led. The others were accustomed to following her, so we herded them to the door and out into the hall. Huge cracks lined the hallway, and we could see the walls beginning to disintegrate.

"Run!" I cried, imagining us crushed by the falling debris, buried under the wreckage of the castle and the water of the lake. We moved as quickly as we could, though my sisters looked back and hesitated at nearly every step. The torches in the hall extinguished themselves, and then even the exhausted princesses ran, in pitch darkness now, careening into walls and tripping over piles of rubble that cascaded from the ceiling and walls. I remembered my light-stick and pulled it from my pocket, concentrating with all my might. The feeble light I produced was enough to keep us from plunging into the crevasse that suddenly opened beneath our feet as the floor cracked apart. Milek pulled Aurelia over the widening crack, and Breckin and I forced the others to leap over it, their skirts swirling around their legs.

Then we reached the drawbridge, and it did not descend for us as it always had in the past. Milek dropped Aurelia's hand, pulled out his sword, and swung hard at the chains that held the bridge. I could not see how a sword could cut through the iron chains, but it did, slicing them as if they were butter, and the bridge fell open with a huge *thump*.

We started across, and we could see that on the other side, beneath the diamond trees, the earth seemed to heave and wriggle. When he got there, Milek ran on, but Breckin and my sisters stopped, and I, bringing up the rear, took an instant to figure out why. The wriggling was not the earth, nor its grasses. It was snakes: the ground was covered in snakes. They hissed and reared up, they rattled their tails and spat. To pass, we would have to walk on them, to crush them beneath our feet, to be bitten and poisoned and surely killed.

"No," Breckin said hoarsely, backing away. The drawbridge shook as the castle fell behind us, piece by piece, and I looked over the edge. Beneath us the water boiled with movement, and I could see the heads of water rats as they swam below, waiting. Their naked pink tails waved above the water, and their horrid snouts poked up, opening and closing, showing razor-sharp little teeth. My knees turned liquid, and I thought I would faint as the bridge swung and rattled beneath me.

"Get off the bridge," I cried shrilly to my sisters, who had pulled up behind me. "There are rats in the moat! Get off!"

Milek had stopped a little ways off and was watching

us. I could barely see his face in the dimness, puzzled and afraid. His lips moved, but I could make out no sound. I felt frozen, powerless to move. Snakes ahead—Breckin's worst fear. Rats below—my worst fear. This could not be happening. It could not!

I said those words again to myself—*It could not. It could not*—and suddenly they made sense to me. The princes had disappeared. They had not been real. The drawbridge chains had melted through. They had not been real. The snakes might not be real, nor the rats. None of this could be happening. None of it was real. I took a deep breath and felt my strength return.

"Hold on to my shoulder," I said to Breckin, taking his hand and placing it there. "Follow me. Look at the light-stick. Don't look down." Then I turned to my sisters, who stood huddled together, trembling, and repeated my words. "Look at my light. Don't look down." I began to walk forward, off the bridge. At my first step onto the ground, I could not help picturing my foot in its leather boot lowering onto the snakes. But I did not look down, and I felt only solid ground beneath my foot. There was nothing coiling itself around my ankle, no sharp fangs piercing my leg. I took another step forward, and another, concentrating on keeping my light strong. I could feel Breckin's hand clamped on my shoulder so hard it hurt, but it helped me to stay focused. I hoped that behind him my sisters followed, hands on one another's shoulders, but I dared not look back to check. Forward I moved through the diamond forest, trying to make out Milek's face in the gloom ahead. I could hear Breckin breathing heavily behind me, and I tried to match my steps to his breath.

As we reached Milek, I heard a strange noise and saw beyond him the golden trees leaning forward toward us, as in a heavy wind. The wind itself struck a moment later. A whirling darkness covered us, and I felt the breath pulled out of me. My light-stick spun out of my hand and away. Objects flew through the air and struck me on my face, my shoulders and chest. I leaned forward, trying to move, but the force of the wind was too strong. Then I felt a hand on my arm and knew it must be Milek's. I turned to grasp the person behind me—was it still Breckin?—and hoped that whoever it was, he or she would do the same to the person behind. We pushed against the wind, pulling one another along. My eyes were closed against the grit that the gale pushed into them. We seemed to move this way, one hard-fought step at a time, for hours, and then suddenly the wind dropped. We were so bent forward against its force that when it ceased, we all fell onto our faces, scraping painfully against the dirt of the path. I lay sobbing and trying to catch my breath, but Milek would not let us rest.

"Up!" he commanded. "You must get up. If we don't get back before daybreak, I don't know if we will ever get back. Zita, Breckin, help me!"

I rubbed the dirt out of my eyes and wobbled to my feet. I could see the silver trees just ahead, and I knew we were almost back. Behind me, my sisters lay sprawled, pale and nearly senseless. I ran to them, urging them to rise, helping each one to her feet. "We're nearly there," I told them, trying to brush grass from their hair, dirt from their faces. "It's almost over. You can rest soon. Just a little farther."

Then I heard a sound that filled me with dread. It was the roar of the wall of water that followed us each time we ran to the enchanted castle. This time it came from the other direction.

"Run!" I screamed, and my sisters heard the terror in my voice, picked up their skirts, and ran. I brought up the rear now, with Breckin and Milek in front. Behind me I could hear the great wave approaching, and I imagined I could feel its spray on my back. My clothes seemed to grow heavy with moisture. *It cannot be real, it cannot,* I said to myself, chanting the words as I ran. My feet sloshed in their wet boots, and my hair dripped into my eyes. Ahead I could see Milek piling the princesses into the dumbwaiter, three—no, four at a time, their wide skirts crushed together to make room. He and Breckin worked the ropes. Up, then down—four more. Up and down, and the last four piled in and disappeared as I ran up. We had done it! They were safe at last—but we were not.

Milek, Breckin, and I turned to face the wall of water that did not exist, and it broke over us with tremendous force. We were tumbled head over heels until there was no way to tell which way was up, but I struck out swimming anyway, kicking off my sodden boots and flailing desperately with my arms. The water was dark and greenish, but I thought I could see a lighter milky green in the distance. I remember feeling that I was thinking very clearly for someone who was drowning, and I thought, *That must be the surface and daylight.* I headed in that direction. My chest burned with the need to breathe. I had to take a breath. I thought, *For an imaginary wave, this one seems very real*, and then I opened my mouth and breathed in. I breathed in water, and I choked and coughed and clawed at my throat in a panic. *It is real,* I told myself. *I should have waited a little longer to breathe. I am dying.* And then I thought no more.

Chapter 12

In Which There Is an Unmasking

erhaps I did die for a moment. I don't know. There was nothingness, and then there was feeling again. If death is nothingness, then I suppose I could have been dead. I do know that waking—or living again—was very terrible. I came to consciousness with lungs full of water and spent a long time retching and coughing until I thought my very insides would rush out of me with the water I expelled. For a time I lay nearly insensible, feeling hard ground beneath me and cold air moving over me. I began to shiver, and I felt something heavy and warm laid over me. I thought about opening my eyes; through my heavy lids I could tell that it was day. But it was just too hard. I slept, or was unconscious again, for a time, and when I woke I heard someone else going through the retching and coughing that I had finished. I felt a great wave of relief but did not know why, and then the reason came to me: Breckin too was alive. He was lying near me, coughing his lungs out on the mossy ground. And Milek? I heard him groan, not far off, and I thought about smiling, but my face was too tired to form itself into any shape at all.

A voice whispered in my ear, "You can sit up now," and so I did. Sitting was as hard as anything I had ever done. I ached all over, arms and legs from swimming, skin from falling and scraping and being pelted with pebbles and sticks in wind and wave, even inside my throat and chest where I had coughed and coughed. I wobbled, and strong arms supported me. I smelled the scent of lemon biscuits and said, "Babette?"

"Oh, my dear," she replied, hugging me. I collapsed into her embrace, noting too late that my sodden clothes were soaking her through. I tried to pull away, but she would not let me, so I rested there against her warmth and strength.

"The others are all right," Babette said at length. "They were not as bad off as you. You took quite a bit of work, my love! I haven't worked like that in three score years or more."

"You did magic on me?" I said weakly. "You healed me?"

"Oh, you're a strong one," Babette said lightly. "It wasn't much, really. But I'm glad to know I still have the skills. Here, let me do something about those bruises." She began to run her hands over my black-and-blue arms, murmuring words I did not recognize. As she touched a spot, the ache there subsided. She did the same to my poor throbbing head, and finally I could focus my eyes and look around me. On the ground nearby, Breckin and Milek lay like waterlogged branches, limp and seemingly lifeless. I must have made a sound of concern, for Babette interrupted her healing to say, "They're all right, love. They're just resting. Gathering their strength."

I nodded. "Where are we?" I asked. I had some idea that we were on a magical isle or the shore of an enchanted lake, but Babette pointed behind me, and I looked out over the water to see our palace shimmering in the sunlight.

"We're on the far side of the lake," she said. "You were thrown here by the wave. It's a good thing it was moving in this direction, and not the other, or the palace would have been swamped by it."

"My sisters—," I started.

"They are all upstairs. Do you remember?"

I recalled the desperate pulls on the dumbwaiter ropes and my great relief just before the wave broke, and I nodded. "And how did you come here?" I asked, stretching out my legs so she could work over them. There was a big gash along my left calf, and I watched with great interest as it began to knit itself. Soon barely a scar remained of it.

"I was tending to my lilacs—you know, they must be pruned in winter, before spring growth begins. And suddenly there was a huge crash, and the whole world seemed to waver before my eyes. I had never seen such a thing before." She paused and asked, "Shall I dry you?"

I nodded, and she passed her hands over my body from head to foot. Liquid cascaded off me as if I were a waterfall, and within moments I was wrung out and perfectly dry. I could feel warmth returning to my hands and feet.

"Go on," I urged her.

"It was obvious that some very strong magic was taking place, and all I could imagine was that it had to do with you. I packed a basket with everything I thought I might need, and I left my cottage for the first time in many years. The forest had grown up so much! I feared I might get lost, but the pull of the magic was very strong. I came to the lake just as the wave hit the shore, and I found the three of you easily enough. And here I am." She nodded and blinked her bright eyes.

"Oh, Babette," I said mournfully. "It was all my fault. I nearly got us all killed. I forgot to hide myself."

"It is all for the best," she said comfortably, patting my head. "Now everything is out in the open. You cannot fight what you cannot see."

"But I still don't *know*," I told her. "I don't know who is doing it, or why."

"I think perhaps you do," Babette replied. "I think that if you look closely, you will see that you know."

"Look closely at what?" I demanded crossly, standing up and brushing ineffectively at my wrinkled skirt.

Babette gave a gesture that could have meant anything or anywhere. I looked around me, at the trees and grasses, still clothed in the brown of winter. I looked at Breckin and Milek, starting to stir now as Babette moved to them and began her healing art. It was neither of them. That I was sure of. I turned to look at the lake, peering into its depths as if I could see the castle far below if I looked hard enough. There was nothing but mud and rock. I looked up at the palace, its faceted windows glimmering in the pale wintry sun. Was she speaking of my father, asking me to look at my father's home? Was this her way of telling me it was he who had tried to kill us all?

I rarely saw the palace from this angle; I had last been on this side of the lake back in spring, when I picked strawberries. From this side, my sisters' bedroom window showed, and I stared at it hard.

"Oh," I said faintly. This was the view that showed in the embroidered coverlet my sisters had made for my twelfth birthday, where I stood at the window and looked out. And there, in the real window, I could see the shadow that had embroidered itself into the coverlet, that Alanna had claimed was spilled chocolate. It was not a spill, I could see that now. It was a face, and it peered out the window, seeming to look right at me. I could see it was not Father. It was a woman, with long hair. I squinted, trying to read the features. They were so familiar, and yet not. Was it Chiara? But Chiara wore her hair up, always in its tight coil. Was it one of my sisters? No, the nose was sharp and the hair dark, not blond. I could see the face clearly now, and I both recognized it and did not. And then in a moment it changed, and wrinkles furrowed the cheeks, the hair grayed, and the features settled into the familiar and beloved face of Nurse. Our own, my sisters' Nurse.

"Oh no," I whispered, clutching at my throat. It was Nurse who had done such wicked things to my poor sisters, who had tried to kill Breckin and Milek and me? How could that be? And *why*? I was filled with horror, and then a moment later I realized, *It was not Father. Oh, thank heaven, it was not Father.*

I spun around to look back at Babette. She was staring up at the window, and I knew that she had seen what I'd seen. We exchanged a look. She nodded to me, and out loud I asked, "But why?"

"I don't know, my dear," Babette answered sadly. "I can't even begin to imagine."

"What shall we do? My sisters are up there with her! They aren't safe. We must get them out!"

Milek sat up with a groan, shaking out his sore limbs. He poked Breckin, who shook his damp red curls till the water drops flew.

"Makes you glad Willem taught us to swim, eh, brother?" Milek said. "I remember cursing him when he threw us in the pond and told us to paddle, but think if he hadn't!"

Breckin laughed weakly, then stared in amazement as Babette dried him as she had me.

"*That's* useful magic," he pointed out. "We could have used some of that under the lake last night."

"It would have done you no good," Babette said tartly. "I couldn't fight against the strength of that. I'm not nearly good enough."

"Then what," I demanded, "are we going to do about Nurse? How shall we break her enchantment if you aren't a good enough witch to do it?"

"Nurse?" Breckin said. "It was Nurse?"

I nodded, and he gaped at me.

"Use Milek's magic to break the enchantment," Babette told me. We stared at her blankly.

"I have no magic, ma'am," Milek said at last. "Only the cloak you gave me, and that's—" He looked around him, but there was no trace of the cloak, torn away by the force of the wave. "That's gone."

Babette smiled gently. "Oh, you have magic," she said. "It's not in spells or potions, but it works just the same. It's been working all along." She and Milek exchanged a look, and he smiled suddenly, a radiant smile that made his weathered face still more handsome.

"Well, then," he said briskly. "We must hurry."

I was bewildered. "But what is our plan? Hurry to do what?"

Milek took my face in his rough hands and looked into my eyes. "Can you trust me to do the best for your sisters, Zita?" he asked. I looked into his deep brown eyes and saw a little of Breckin there. I knew then that he would do everything he could, and that I could trust him. I nodded.

"Just tell me what to do," I said.

We made our way around the edge of the lake to the land bridge, struggling through thorny bushes and tall grasses. When we got to the bridge, I said to Babette, "She will see us crossing. She watches the bridge."

"I know," Babette replied. "I want her to see us."

"*You're* coming in?" Breckin asked her, astonished. "What if the king finds out? What will Nurse do to you?"

Babette shrugged. "I have no idea. But now that she knows who I am, there is no point in hiding. I want to pull her out, bring her to us. We need to unmask her."

I thought of the face I had seen in the window— young, dark-eyed and dark-haired, beautiful in a cold, harsh way—and then a moment later old and wrinkled, the face of a beloved servant. Which was the mask? When the disguise was removed, what face would be revealed?

We marched across the bridge and were met by a guard. He was much larger than any guard I had seen there before, and I did not recognize him. He held a lance before us, and I could see a sword and a knife at his side.

"Halt," he commanded us. We stopped, unnerved by the sharp point of the lance.

I stepped forward, nearly impaling myself on the point. "I am Zita, King Aricin's daughter," I said in as imperious a voice as I could muster. "Stand aside."

The guard snorted but did not reply, and he did not move. I held my breath and stepped forward, expecting to feel the painful push of the lance against my breast-bone. But the lance passed right through me, and the guard wavered as the princes had the night before, and disappeared.

"Oh, very good, Zita!" Babette said approvingly. "Your Nurse is excellent at illusion. I would not have guessed."

"I didn't recognize him," I told her. "I knew there had been no new servants but Milek hired this month."

"It can be useful, being a princess and a serving girl," Breckin teased, poking me. I swatted at his hand, swallowing the fear I'd felt when I stepped into the lance.

We started up the stairs nervously, unsure what threat might leap out at us from behind each tapestry or curtain. On the landing of the second floor, there was a sudden hiss and flapping, and a great number of bats swooped down from the ceiling. I shrieked and ducked and covered my head, sure that the nasty things—rats with wings!—would tangle themselves in my hair.

"They're nothing, Zita!" Breckin reminded me, pulling me upright. "Just an illusion." We moved on, up the marble stairs, but the distance from stair to stair began to grow greater. Soon we were clambering from one step to the next, and then leaping, and then we had to boost one another up to the next stair. I stopped, panting, after one such climb, and looked behind us. The staircase seemed to drop off below to nothingness, as if we were looking over the edge of an enormous cliff. Milek followed my gaze and wobbled a bit on the step. I grabbed his arm.

"I don't much like heights," he admitted, steadying himself.

"It's just a staircase," I reminded him. "It isn't real."

"This climb surely *feels* real," he said, laughing, and I laughed too, weakly.

At last we reached the top floor, and I looked down the hall toward my sisters' room. As the staircase had become endlessly high, so the hall was now endlessly long, the far end wreathed in fog or smoke. Sighing, we set out down the corridor, moving as quickly as we could.

Miles and miles we trudged, or so it felt. I was confused: we were walking and walking, so it couldn't be an illusion, could it? But it couldn't be real, either, for I knew perfectly well that our hallway was not ten miles long. It made my brain ache to think about it.

Then, finally, we stood outside my sisters' door. I reached out to hammer on the door, fearful of what was taking place within, but Babette stopped my hand.

We listened for a moment; there was no sound from inside. Then Milek put his face close to the door, spoke Aurelia's name, and began to talk.

I could not tell you exactly what he said. It was a song and a poem and a story, a tapestry of a tale, woven with strands of fear and magic and love. He spoke for Aurelia's ears, though we did not know whether she could hear on the other side of the door. He told of our adventure beneath the lake, again as if it were a dream he'd had. He described the dance, reminding Aurelia of her beauty and of his love for her, and then he told of the cock's crow and the terrifying disintegration of the castle. He recounted the disappearance of the princes, and I thought I heard a muffled gasp from within the chamber. He told of our terror over the snakes and the water rats, of the terrible wind, and then he described the wave that had taken and nearly killed us. When he was done, there was silence for a long, long time.

Finally, Milek spoke once more. "Aurelia," he called gently, but loudly enough to be heard within. "Aurelia, I nearly lost my life for love of you. Would you have been sad if I were gone?"

The answer came immediately. I could hear the strength in Aurelia's voice through the thick door as she cried out, "Oh, my dearest, if you had died, I would have died as well!"

The chamber door flew open with a crash, and from within came a cry of wrath and despair that nearly shattered my heart. I ran inside, and Milek and Breckin and Babette followed suit. There were my sisters, sitting up in their beds, their faces flushed and their eyes alert for the first time in months. And there, at the end of the passage between the rows of beds, stood Nurse, the young Nurse who had shown herself in the window, not the old woman whom I thought I had known. She was in a terrible fury, and her wrath was horrible to see.

Nurse stood waiting for us, and I stumbled to a halt when I saw her. If I could have run backward out the door and away, I think I would have. But as I turned, I saw Milek bending to the bed where Aurelia now sat up. Her arms went around him, her lovely face turned up to his, and I realized that there was no turning back.

Then Nurse saw Babette, bringing up the rear, and her face changed and rearranged itself once more. A crafty look came into her eyes, and her voice when she spoke was nearly a purr.

"Well, Babette," she said. "It has been a long time indeed. I did not think we would meet again."

"Do I know you?" Babette asked politely.

"Perhaps not," Nurse said. "But I know you. Was it not you who gave a gift to the princess Aurelia at her christening?"

Babette smiled gently. "How could that be?" she said. "Witches and all magic were banned from the kingdom when the dear child was born."

"Because I made it so!" Nurse cried out. "Because I did not want the queen protected! Because I wanted . . ." She stopped.

"So it was you," Babette said musingly. "How did you do it?"

Nurse frowned. "I convinced the king it would be safer. He knew the old stories—the dangers of the angry witch, the jealous witch at the christening. He knew his daughter would be beautiful and beloved—a perfect target. What father would run that risk?"

"But I came anyway," Babette pointed out.

Nurse snorted. "I did not know until it was too late. I saw you enter, but you were just an old woman. And you were by the cradle before I realized the illusion—and it was too late."

"I protected her," Babette said. She sounded proud and rather pleased with herself.

"What did you use?" Nurse asked.

"The Protection of Love," Babette told her. "Do you know that charm? The more she is loved, the stronger the shield. And when she is loved by someone with his whole heart, and he would give his life for her, no spell can hold her."

Nurse glared at her. I could feel her gaze burning past me, and I felt a sudden pain in my arm. I looked down at my sleeve. It was smoldering. I turned to see Babette's apron burst into flames, and without thinking I grabbed a quilt off the nearest bed and threw it around her. Smoke rose up, but the fire was out. I could feel Babette trembling through the quilt. The room was silent.

Then Nurse spun around, and everywhere her gaze landed, there fire broke out. In a moment the bedclothes on every bed were ablaze, and my sisters screamed and tried to flee as their hair and nightdresses caught fire.

"Use the blankets!" Milek shouted. "Wrap the blankets around yourselves! Drop down and crawl!"

Those of us unscathed beat the flames out on the others, and the horrid smell of burned hair rose up. The room began to fill with smoke. Then I heard Babette's voice speaking words I did not know. There was a crash of thunder—indoors?—and suddenly rain began beating down on us from a dark cloud that hovered near the ceiling. The flames were out in a moment, and the room silent but for the coughing and crying of my sisters. I pushed between the beds to one of the windows and flung it open, gasping for breath as cold, clean air blew in.

When I turned, I saw that Nurse was herself again, the wrinkled old woman whom we had loved all our lives. The bedchamber was destroyed, a mess of charred bedding and water. The beds ran with rainwater; my sisters' hair dripped down their backs, and their night-clothes clung to them. Asenka, who was closest to me as I stood by the window, reached out her hand to me, and I grasped it tightly. I could feel her shaking. Suddenly I was very angry, and my anger made me reckless.

"Why have you done this, Nurse?" I shouted. "Look at us! You have nearly killed my sisters. Why would you do such a thing?"

"I?" Nurse said sweetly, her voice calm and measured, as it was when she soothed my sisters to sleep when they had the toothache. "I see only one witch in this room. I would not harm my darlings, would I, Alima?" She turned to Alima, and taking a handkerchief from her apron pocket, where she always kept one, she dabbed the water from Alima's face. Alima turned to me, her expression blank with confusion.

"It's only Nurse," she said. "She wouldn't hurt us. You know she wouldn't! What reason could she have?"

"I think I know," Babette said. "I believe, after all these years, I have figured it out."

Nurse bustled up the corridor between the rows of beds toward Babette. She looked fierce, but fierce as

Nurse looked when one of my sisters would not go to bed on time, not fierce as the witch who had set fire to the room had looked. "I think you should leave, madam," she said to Babette. "I think you are not wanted here. We must clean up this terrible mess you have made and get these girls to bed. They've been ill." She reached Aurelia's bed. Aurelia now stood beside it, wet as a newborn kitten, and she clutched Milek's arm tightly.

Nurse frowned mightily. "Young man," she scolded him, "you are not allowed in the princesses' bedchamber. Kindly remove yourself, and be certain that I will speak to the butler about this. And you too," she said to Breckin, who stood near the door, his red hair dripping.

Nobody moved. Nurse began to swell up the way she did when she was annoyed, and we all shrank back, not knowing whether she would turn into the other Nurse again, setting fire to all that moved. She did not. She stayed our Nurse, sputtering and scolding, and I could see my sisters looking more and more unsure of themselves as she ordered them hither and thither—"Dry your hair, princesses! Come, let me find you clean nightclothes! My dears, come away from the window, you'll catch your death!" Only Aurelia stood firm, her hand in Milek's.

"Sisters," she said, "we must go." Her voice was commanding, and even I felt I should obey. The other eleven collected themselves and scooted over sodden mattresses, squelched over soaked carpets, to join Aurelia at the door. Nurse was now back at the window, and I watched her brow wrinkle in a frown. She was not used to being disobeyed; for more than two score years she had ruled the bedchamber.

"Girls—," she said, but Aurelia interrupted her.

"We have nothing more to say to you," she informed Nurse coolly. "We will be sure Father hears of this. He will deal with you."

"Hears of what?" My father's voice came, unexpected, and several of my sisters gave little shrieks as they saw him at the door. He surveyed the wreckage of the bedchamber, and his gray eyebrows rose on his forehead. "What on earth—," he managed. We stood stock-still, all of us, unsure of which way to move. It was fascinating to see his face as he registered all that the chamber contained. He saw his daughters standing, flushed and dripping, and years dropped from him as he realized that they were awake and alive and, more, that they were well. He saw the fire damage and the water damage, and a wave of confusion and dismay passed over him. He saw Milek and Breckin—men in his daughters' bedchamber!—and fury took hold of him. Before he could gather his wits together to speak, though, Babette came forward.

"Your Majesty," she said, and sank in a deep curtsy.

"Who are you, woman?" he said rudely. "What do you here, in my daughters' chamber?"

"Perhaps you will remember me from the christening of your firstborn, Aurelia," Babette said to him. Father looked at her, and looked again. I could see him try to recall; then all at once he remembered.

"You are the witch," he proclaimed. "I had you banished—I had all of you banished! You were nearly killed when you appeared that day."

"But your wife intervened for me," Babette reminded him. "Because she and I were old friends; because I loved her. Do you remember?"

"I remember," Father said in a low voice. "I spared you for Amara's sake. But she is not here now."

"There was another witch at that christening," Babette told him. "The spell I cast was for protection only. The other cast a spell as well, though we did not know."

"Another witch?" Father said, confused. "There was no one there! Just Amara and the baby, and myself, and the priest, and Nurse. And you, of course."

"Yes," said Babette.

There was a long silence, and then, as one, we turned to look at Nurse. Caught off guard, she was staring at

Father. The longing in her eyes was palpable, and I drew a deep breath. It seemed strange, inappropriate in such an old woman, to see such adoration. Then, for a moment, Nurse's features wavered, and we could see again the young, beautiful woman, the witch, beneath the illusion. Father gasped and staggered back, his hand to his mouth.

"Taika," he whispered.

"Ah," said Nurse. "You do remember." She seemed to shimmer for a moment, and then her age fell away from her, starting with her hair, which became dark and shining, then her face, which unwrinkled as if an iron were passing over it. Her complexion brightened, her cheeks grew pink, her eyes sparkled. Her furrowed neck, her heavy breasts and thick waist smoothed and slimmed, and then the change was done. She stood before us, a dark-haired, gleaming beauty. There was nothing of our aged Nurse left in her.

"He loved you once," Babette said softly. Nurse—Taika—turned on her fiercely.

"He loves me still!" she cried.

"No," Father said. "No. That was long ago. That was lifetimes ago."

"I have never stopped," Taika told him, eyes flashing. "I have remained faithful all these years."

"I was a boy!" Father protested. "I loved you as a boy

loves, Taika. Then I met my wife, and it was she I loved as a man."

"No," Taika said. Her voice was low and throaty.

"Yes," Father insisted. "If you had come to me, I would have told you."

"But I was with you all along," Taika said in silky tones. "As your wife bore only daughters, naught but girl after girl, I was there to comfort you. As she weakened and wizened and all but disappeared, who was it but I who held your hand and patted your brow and consoled you? When she died, who raised your children? And who made sure they would stay with you and not desert you for another man?" With a start I remembered the silent dinners with the princes who had come to call, my sisters' inability to speak or even look at the men who courted them.

Father gave a cry then, and I felt terrible sorrow for him. What had this woman done, out of her twisted love?

"You prevented me from having sons?"

Taika said nothing, but she smiled.

"But. . . ," I protested. "Babette, you said—"

"I know," Babette told me. "I said there were few of us who could have that effect. Taika is one who could. She should not have. It could not end well."

I looked at Father, and he looked back at me. For the

first time—for the only time—he truly looked at me, and I felt that he saw me. Me, Zita, the last-born of his children, his own true daughter; not Zita, the creature who had killed his beloved wife. Now the one who really had killed her was exposed. The witch had caused my mother to have only daughters so that Father would cast his queen aside. I watched this knowledge dawn on Father's face and saw that he knew he too was at fault for wanting a son so desperately. Between them, Taika and he had driven my mother to her death. In Father's haunted eyes, I saw at last that he knew I was not to blame, and that he blamed himself.

"Zita," he said hoarsely. "Daughter, forgive me."

I moved to his side, my tears spilling over, and for the first time he put his arms around me. His embrace was a place of such strength and safety that I felt I might never be afraid again. But too soon he released me.

And then he turned to Nurse, to Taika.

"How could you?" he asked, his voice a mixture of bewilderment and anger.

"How could I not?" she said. "I loved you, don't you understand? I waited, and I waited. Even after she died, you did not see me. I had thought her death would end it."

"End the love I had for her?" he said. "Then you are a fool."

"Oh, I am that," she agreed. "For then you saw only your daughters. The little love you had left, you gave to them. There was nothing for me—nothing! I couldn't bear it. I couldn't bear it! And then you threatened to dismiss me. 'They do not need a nurse,' you said! I could not go. How could I leave you? So I had them dance, and they sickened, and you needed me more and more. And then I thought maybe, if they were not there anymore, you might—"

Aurelia cried, "Nurse!" with a voice full of pain.

But Taika was not Nurse, not anymore. She never really had been. This was too much for Aurelia and my other sisters, who had loved Nurse, and they covered their faces against her, weeping. But she turned away from them and looked only at our father, hoping against all hope.

I turned to look, too, and I saw the fury that we all dreaded spilling over him in a wild rush. At last fear crossed Taika's face. As Father advanced on her, she backed down the space between the rows of beds, and her arms came up as if to ward off a blow. But Father did not hit her. He wouldn't. I knew he would never hit a woman, though she was a sorceress. Instead, in a low voice that trembled with anger and horror, he said, "Witch, what have you done?"

Taika sank almost to her knees, her power weakened

by her love for Father. But before she came entirely down, she remembered herself and reared up again, her own anger mounting.

"You will not have me, after all?" she cried, and her voice rose to a shriek. "I am not good enough for you? Then no one shall ever have you!" She moved her arms in a wild pattern and spoke strange words, and Babette let out a cry. I heard the same terrible crash that had so frightened us in the castle below the lake, and when I looked upward I saw cracks appear in the ceiling and felt a light rain of plaster on my hair. My sisters screamed. The walls seemed to shake. From belowstairs I heard shouts of terror from the servants.

"Come!" Milek called at the door of the bedchamber. "Hurry!"

Breckin ran to me and grabbed my hand, but I turned to my father, thinking to beg him to escape with us. I could see no fear in his face as he watched Taika work her magic, only a calm resolve, and I heard him say, very clearly, "My dear, my dearest dust; I come, I come." They were the words from the poem I had read, about the lover who longed to join his beloved in death. He was speaking to my mother, and I feared that there was no hope for him. Then he turned to us and said, "Go, daughters. Now! I cannot hold her off for long." He started toward the witch and grasped her hands, trying to stop whatever destruction she was trying to wreak as she wove her spells in the air.

My sisters protested, sobbing and calling out to him, but his mouth, no longer twisted, was set in a firm line, and his resolve too was firm. Again he said only, "Go!" And so we went, rushing from the room, leaving my father and Taika facing each other as he gripped her arms and she struggled to escape, speaking dreadful words in an unknown language. Down the hallway—once again its usual length—we raced, and down the stairs, now their usual height. At each door we gathered together servants and Father's councillors, all terrified, all fleeing from some horror we could not name. At the entrance to the land bridge we stood—Breckin, Milek, my sisters, and I—making sure everyone—serving girls and footmen, Cook and Chiara and the weaselly Burle—got across safely before we stepped on. The servants watched in horror as the lake beneath us began to heave, and we struggled to stay upright.

The bridge swayed and cracked, and I looked around wildly for Babette. Then I saw her, staggering down the marble staircase. She was so pale, I feared she would faint.

"Where is Father?" Aurelia cried.

"You cannot help him, my dear," Babette told her. "Come, we must get across the bridge. Hurry!"

We began to cross, but the lake heaved again, and the bridge was submerged. We had to retreat back into the palace. "The boats!" I cried. "To the boats!" We ran down into the lower level to a small door that opened directly onto the water. Tied up there were the little rowboats that my sisters took out on occasion to paddle around the lake. We scrambled into them as the walls and towers shivered above us. I climbed into the last boat, and Milek, who had handed me in, climbed in after me.

We set out across the lake, a flock of pastel-colored boats like so many ducks in a line. Partway across, the wind picked up, and waves began to slap beneath us. A terrible noise sounded behind me. With my sisters, I turned to look back at the palace. I saw the waters of the lake behind us rise straight upward in a waterspout, and the wind caught it and whirled it around and around. Suddenly I remembered the dream I'd once had, on the day I'd met Breckin, of my sisters caught on the lake, and the terrible storm, and the waterspout that threatened to carry them off. I cringed in fear.

But this was not my dream. The water rose up and up, washing over the palace, through the open windows of even my sisters' high tower room, where my father and Taika remained. Then, with a roar, the lake water came straight down again, and the wind died, and everything was quiet. We cried out, all of us, to see that the lake itself was gone now, and only a wide, sparkling stream remained. It wound around the marble supports that held the palace up, and the smell of it, clean and fresh, made me realize how thick and stagnant the lake had been.

Fearful of what we might find, we rowed back, moving swiftly with the current that now ran past the palace, and climbed through the door back inside. What we saw stunned us. There was nothing left. The water had swept through, taking with it chairs and tables and wall hangings, ovens and carpets and paintings. The mold that had rimed the walls too was gone. The whole palace was washed clean, as if it had just been built.

Leaving the others to marvel over this, Aurelia and I clasped hands and began to climb the staircase up to the bedchamber. We both knew, I think, what we would see, but it was a shock nevertheless to push open the door and find . . . nothing. My sisters' hairbrushes and mirrors, their little tubs of creams and bottles of perfume, their jewel boxes—all had vanished. Not a dress in the closet, not one of the twelve beds that had lined the walls was left. And no sign, no sign at all, of Nurse, or of our father.

"Oh, Aurelia," I said mournfully. "Is he gone, then?"

"I fear he is," she replied softly. "Poor Father!"

"I think it is what he wanted, though," I mused.

"Is it? How do you know?"

I reminded her of what Father had said at the last: "My dearest dust; I come, I come."

"He wanted to be with Mother," I explained. "He loved only her."

Tears stood in Aurelia's eyes as she hugged me. "That is not so," she said fiercely, giving me a little shake. "He loved her most—that is true. Perhaps he loved her too much. But he loved us all, in his way."

"Even me?" I asked.

She looked down at me and smiled through her tears. "Silly Zita," she said fondly. "Even you. You were the last of us he held. Could you not feel that he loved you? And although he longed for Mother, I do not think he wanted to die. He stayed and defied the witch so we could escape. How could he have loved us more?"

I thought of Father's arms around me, that first and last embrace, and I sensed that Aurelia was right. It was strange, and perhaps unseemly, but I felt a swell of happiness pass through me that I had never known before. I had lost my father, but I had also gained my father, and I knew I would never lose him completely again.

Chapter 13

In Which My Story Does Not End

e mourned Father deeply for a time, dressing in black and then in muted colors with black armbands. We did not celebrate Christmas that year. But we were busy, too, for the gutted, soggy palace had to be thoroughly dried and completely refurbished, from bottom to top. Aurelia, now queen—though she chose not to have a coronation to disturb our mourning—oversaw the choice of all the fittings. The result was rooms of uncommon grace and beauty. All the work was local, from the tapestries woven on looms in nearby Walderen Town to the colored goblets blown at the Mirven glassworks near the border with Blaire. The people were happy to have the work, and well paid for doing it, and their fondness for their queen seemed to grow daily.

My sisters and I now each had a private bedchamber, for Aurelia opened up all the unused rooms and furnished them anew. In my own room, however, I felt very lonely. Immediately I invited Anisa to share with me, and she must have felt as I did, for immediately she moved her things in. In short order my other sisters had done the same, and we had a veritable round-robin of sleeping arrangements, with sisters moving from room to room as the whim struck. It was glorious. At last I was truly a member of my own family.

My sisters quickly learned to love Babette, and we invited her to live with us in the palace. She laughed and refused. "I have lived my whole life in my own little cottage, and there I will stay," she told us. But she removed the illusion of ruin from it, and my sisters and I soon wore a path from our palace to the cottage, where Babette always had a tray of sweets and pot of tea ready for us.

Aurelia and Milek were inseparable. They held hands as if their palms were sewn together, and they laughed and whispered together in a way that was lovely to see. None of us were the least surprised when, after several fortnights, Aurelia announced that she and Milek would marry.

"He does not want to be king," she told us as we sat beside the kitchen fire, toasting chestnuts. The firelight flickered on her hair, and the joy in her face made her even more beautiful. "He will be prince consort, and I will rule with him by my side."

As spring came on and the days lengthened, we spent our time in a blur of dress fittings for the wedding, consultations with bakers and chefs, dance lessons (for me—my sisters already danced perhaps too well), and hours spent with specialists in the beauty trade. I was slathered with lotions and unguents in an attempt to tame my wild hair, smooth my skin (roughened from years of scullery work), and fade my tanned and freckled face to pristine whiteness. It did no discernable good, but I felt much more like a princess. I threw myself into the whirlwind of preparations for the wedding, so busy that I did not have time to think of anything beyond whether Aurelia should have pearls woven through her braided hair or a diadem of sapphires to circle her head. We chose the pearls as being more youthful.

A week or so before the wedding, Breckin and Milek's mother came. I was nervous to meet her at first, but she was lively and kindhearted, and we got on at once. She wanted to see the kitchen, and I took her to the vast, cheerful space where Cook reigned. It was a far different place from the dank, smoky kitchen it had once been. Bright copper pans hung from the ceiling, and the smell of baking bread made our mouths water. Melita, for that was Breckin's mother's name, *ooh*ed and *aah*ed in wonder, and Cook was more than pleased at her admiration.

The day of the wedding dawned bright and warm. It was early June, a perfect morning, with a cloudless sky and warm breezes. Except for Aurelia, we girls dressed together, rushing to the window every few minutes to see which guests had arrived and what they wore.

"Who are they?" Asmita asked, pointing as four handsome young men climbed out of a carriage, then handed out an older, white-haired woman whose lavender velvet dress fit her badly.

Ariadne gave a cry. "Oh! That is Queen Eleanora and her sons! Remember them, Althea?" I recalled the story of King Damon and his dowdy queen and their four sons, and my father's fury after their visit, his desperate desire for a son of his own.

"I remember," Althea said. "Oh, they have grown even more handsome. Have none of them married?"

"It seems not," I said with a wicked grin. "I think they are ripe for the picking, sisters!"

My sisters were dizzy with the excitement of finally meeting men who might be suitors—and being able to speak to them. For days they had bathed in milk to silken their skin, washed their hair in cold spring water to bring out its shine, and whitened their faces with lemon. Their satin dresses were all in shades of blue (though Alanna pouted that blue did not flatter her, as her eyes were nearer to gray). I was also in blue, but it was closer to green, like the sea in a place that is very warm. My earrings were drops of aquamarine, and looking at them in the mirror, I remembered when Aurelia had pierced my ears and told me that now I, too, was a real princess. In the big mirror I could see my jewel-festooned silver shoes peeping out from beneath my dress. They pinched a bit, accustomed as I was to leather boots, but they were beautiful, and they were just like my sisters', so I loved them.

When we were done admiring ourselves, we went in to Aurelia. She stood alone in the center of her room. Her gown was ivory satin, as pale and creamy as her skin, and it was woven through with pearls. The bodice was tight, buttoned up the back with a row of tiny pearl buttons, and its long sleeves, buttoned too with pearls, came to points over her hands. She had left her hair unbraided, and it cascaded simply down her back. A circlet of pearls rested on her brow, and her blue eyes shone.

We circled her, chattering away, and she stood quietly in the middle, every inch a queen.

"Happy is the bride the sun shines upon," quoted Amina.

"Oh, I would be as happy if it were sleeting!" Aurelia said. She twirled around, showing us her gown, and then threw her arms around me.

"Thank you, Zita," she whispered to me.

"For what?" I asked.

"For . . . oh, for everything. For helping us. For saving us. And most of all, for bringing me Milek."

"Oh," I said, nonplussed. "That. Well, you're welcome."

She laughed, and I laughed with her, glad to see her blissful after so many years of quiet despair. Then a knock sounded at the door, and Anisa answered it. Babette came in, carrying a tissue-wrapped package.

"No, Babette," Aurelia protested. "No gifts from you. You have given me so much already."

"It is not really a gift, my dear," Babette said, placing her hand gently on Aurelia's cheek. "And it is not really from me." She unwrapped the package and pulled out a length of ivory lace, intricately woven with flowers and vines. It was exquisite.

"This was your mother's wedding veil," Babette told Aurelia, and Aurelia gasped. "She gave it to me for safekeeping long, long ago—before you were born."

"Oh, Babette," Aurelia breathed. She held up the

lace, admiring it, and then turned so Babette could attach it to her pearl diadem. "Just fasten it in back," Aurelia directed. "I want nothing hiding my face. I want to see everything today."

The lace veil was perfect with Aurelia's gown, and the glitter of tears in her eyes as she admired it in the mirror only made her more beautiful. We were all silent now, looking at her and thinking how our mother must have looked when she was a bride herself. From the portraits and tapestries that once hung in the palace— all lost now—it had been clear to see that she had looked very much like Aurelia. I thought then of my father, and Aurelia must have been thinking the same thing, for she said, "How I wish Father were here to walk me down the aisle!"

Hesitantly, for I did not wish to spoil Aurelia's joy on her wedding day, I asked, "What is your earliest memory of Father?"

Aurelia was silent for a moment, thinking. Finally she spoke. "I was very, very little," she said. "I think it is my first memory at all. Mother had gone riding, and I was trying to see her out the window. I was too little. Father had been out hunting, and when he noticed me, he picked me up and swung me around. I remember he smelled like spring. Like fresh air. He lifted me so I could see, and we watched Mother come out of the stables on her horse. Father held me tight. He was so strong. . . ." Aurelia closed her eyes.

Allegra spoke up. "I remember he gave me a gift once. A fur-trimmed muff. It was so tiny—just right to keep my hands warm. It must have been a name-day gift. He kissed the top of my head when he gave it to me."

I felt my throat swell.

One by one, my sisters told their earliest memories of our father. Alima, then Amina, Akila, Asenka, Adena, Althea, Ariadne, Alanna, Asmita, Anisa. As they spoke, I held tight to the memory of Father handing the book of poetry to me, of Father's arms around me for the first and last time.

When all the girls had spoken, Aurelia stood and came over to me. She held out her hands, and I put mine in hers. "Do you know what else I remember?" she asked me. I shook my head.

"It was when you were about six. You were in the hallway, arguing with one of the fire boys that Cook always kept on hand. Father and I watched as you gave him the most wonderful tongue-lashing. I don't know what he'd done to you, but it must have been something quite terrible. You called him an addled fool and the son of a donkey and told him that if he were any more stupid, he'd set fire to his own head."

My sisters snorted with laughter. I didn't remember

this, but it certainly sounded like something I'd do.

"Father was laughing and laughing. I couldn't tell you when I'd seen him laugh, before or since. He said, 'She is a real firebrand! She reminds me of myself, that one.'"

The room was suddenly filled with the snifflings and gulpings that thirteen girls make when they are trying not to cry. In a moment, though, Babette clapped her hands, breaking the spell cast by the memory of our parents. "Princesses, are you ready?" she said. "I think it is nearly time."

Aurelia adjusted her veil, and I bent and straightened her train.

"I am ready," she said.

And so it happened that my eldest sister was married at last, in the chapel of our palace. She walked herself down the aisle, and her pace was steady and controlled, her smile a beacon. Milek waited for her in full dress uniform, his beard neatly trimmed, looking tremendously handsome. Beside him stood only Breckin, who had cleaned up very nicely. His hair had been cut and his hands, for the first time since I'd known him, were white and clean.

We girls lined up beside Aurelia, so the thirteen of us were in a row, and I knew then that for me, thirteen was the luckiest of numbers. Through a daze of happy tears I heard the traditional marriage vows, heard Aurelia's firm "I do" and Milek's "Yes! I do!," so enthusiastic that many in the chapel pews chuckled. When the priest pronounced them husband and wife, they kissed, and their faces when they turned to face the congregation were radiant. They practically ran back down the aisle, and we crowded after them cheering and throwing rose petals that fell like snow and scented the air deliciously.

After the ceremony, the guests repaired to the ballroom, its great door opened for the first time since before I was born. The floor of inlaid wood shone, and the room was adorned with new tapestries and lighted with silver candelabra, perfect for a party. An orchestra played lively tunes, and servants circulated with plates of delicacies and peach- and raspberry-flavored champagnes. I took a glass, and after I drank I could feel the bubbles rising up in me so that I felt I was nearly floating. I looked around for Breckin but did not see him, so I danced and danced with anyone who asked me, watching my sisters chattering away to the lords and princes who partnered them, able at last to talk and, apparently, making up quite well for lost time.

Suddenly my eyes were drawn toward the entrance of the ballroom, and I stopped dead in the middle of an intricate dance step. My partner stumbled, nearly crushing my toes, but I ignored his apologies, dropped his hand, and skimmed across the floor to greet Breckin as he stood surveying the crowd, searching, I hoped, for me.

I stopped in front of him and curtsied, and he bowed. Then he looked me up and down. I was very glad I was dressed in satin and festooned with jewels, for his face lit up in appreciation and his smile pleased me greatly.

"Shall we dance?" he asked, bowing.

I grinned. "I would be honored, sir—if you think we can stop dancing at the end of the song!" Then I laughed, and joy bubbled up in me so strongly that I spun in a circle, making Breckin laugh as well. When I faced him again, I heard the musicians begin to play, a soft, slow measure. Breckin held out his hand.

My eyes on Breckin, and his on me, we stepped onto the dance floor. I placed my hand in his, and he put his arm around my waist. We waltzed together with a grace I would never have guessed we possessed. At the end of the dance we stopped, breathless, and I suddenly was overcome with shyness.

"And how is it, being a princess?" Breckin asked me as we made our way to the edge of the floor.

"Oh," I said, my eyes downcast, "it is wonderful. And very strange—perhaps too strange."

"Too strange?"

I took a deep breath and looked squarely at him. "I am still Zita, you know. I cannot stop being her, no matter how finely I am dressed or how many jewels are placed around my neck. I am still the serving maid, the baker, the cook's assistant, even though I am raised to my sisters' equal." I remembered then something Babette had told me. *Zita means "little rose,"* she had said. *And it means "seeker."* It was true at last. I was all those things. I was Zita the servant, the baker. I was Zita the rose, in my blue-green dress with my red hair. And I was Zita the seeker, who had sought and found her family and her future.

In reply Breckin bent his head to mine, and our lips touched in the kiss that had been forbidden to me since I'd made my vow to Aurelia that I would not be kissed before she was. Now she was married and would be kissed regularly, and I was free.

The wedding cake, which Cook and I had baked with just a little help from Babette, was cut and parceled out and proclaimed delicious. Then the bride and groom were bundled into a white carriage drawn by two snow-white horses and carried off on their honeymoon to the seaside, where Aurelia had never been. Of course, she had never been anywhere, and I could only hope that this little trip was the first of many she and Milek, who had been everywhere during his soldiering, would take as queen and prince consort.

The guests stayed till the dawn light showed in the east, and my sisters and I bade them good-bye at the door. Breckin kissed my hand there, like a courtier, and my sisters saw us and laughed and teased us with delight. Several noblemen and princes from the neighboring kingdoms had asked to call on them the following week, and they were more pleased than I can say. We did not go to sleep after everyone had left, but retired to the largest bedroom and gathered on the two beds. There we sprawled, brushing out one another's hair and nibbling on canapés left over from the evening.

"The most beautiful bride," Adena said. "Wasn't she?"

We all agreed.

"Do you think I can wear the veil when I marry?" Alanna said dreamily. She had danced half the night in the arms of one of King Damon's sons, and he had asked to call again a fortnight hence.

"I think we all should wear it," Allegra proclaimed. "Each in order, and you at the end, Zita!" I smiled at the thought, imagining the lace perched atop my red curls, and then yawned widely, starting a series of yawns that passed in turn from one sister to the next.

Our gossip went on for a time, but one by one voices

dropped out of it, until only I remained awake. For a time I watched them slumber, my beloved sisters, in the pale light of the moon that came in through the tall windows. And as sleep claimed me as well, I knew that at long last I was where I belonged, safe and snug in my own happily ever after.

❧DIANE ZAHLER❧

has always loved fairy tales. As a little girl, she pored over picture books about evil stepmothers and magic charms. At her first job in the children's room at the public library, she sneaked stories of witches and their curses from the shelves and hid in corners to savor them. Working in children's book publishing, she seized any fairy tales that passed by her desk and took them home to read. When she wrote textbooks, she slipped princesses and enchantments into lessons on action verbs and serial commas. Now she lives with her husband, son, and dog in New York's Harlem Valley, in an old farmhouse held together by magic spells and duct tape, writing fairy tales of her own.

For exclusive information
on your favorite authors and artists,
visit www.authortracker.com.